A Cliché Christmas

10/14

Nicole Deese

Letting Go Series
All For Anna
All She Wanted
All Who Dream

A Cliché Christmas

Nicole Deese

Waterfall
PRESS

Text copyright © 2014 Nicole Deese

Published by Waterfall Press, Grand Haven, MI

www.brilliancepublishing.com

ISBN-13: 9781477826171
ISBN-10: 1477826173

Cover design by Kerri Resnick

Library of Congress Control Number: 2014942338

Printed in the United States of America

To my friends and family in Oregon.
No matter where I land,
my home will always be with you.

CHAPTER ONE

I glared at the incessant blinking of my cursor and groaned.
Eleven months of the year, I lived in a perpetual state of holly-jolly fanfare. But by the time the first of November rolled around, I was completely Christmased out. I know I sound like a Scrooge to admit such a travesty, but believe me, when you build a career on Christmas cheer and holiday hype, the warm fuzzies of nostalgia fade faster than Hollywood's latest scandal.

When I wrote my first Christmas pageant at nineteen, I had no idea I was actually sealing my fate. But seven years, a few dozen screenplays, and three Hallmark movies later, Christmas had become exactly that. My destiny.

Ironically, December was my only month off. And I took full advantage of those blessed four weeks, which magically buoyed me for another year of fa-la-la-la-la-ing.

Since I had moved to LA seven years ago, my Nan—short for both Nancy and Nana—and I had traveled to a new tropical destination each year, enjoying sunshine instead of snow, and hulas instead of caroling. Last Christmas it was a two-week Caribbean cruise, but this year our nontraditional holiday extravaganza would be a remote getaway in the Hawaiian Islands.

Clicking out of my latest work in progress, entitled *Noelle's First Noel*, I navigated through my newest temptation to procrastinate, a travel website that flung me into a cyclone of palm trees, sandy beaches, fruity drinks, and—

My phone did the cha-cha across my desk.

Nan.

Today was Tuesday—volunteer day at the senior center. She never called on Tuesdays.

An alarming icy-hot sensation crawled up my throat. I grabbed my cell. "Nan?"

"Georgia! I'm so glad you answered."

The balloon of air I was holding inside my chest released. "Hey, are you okay?"

"Oh, I'm fine, darlin'. But I did just hear some distressing news."

"Is it Mom?" The muscles across my shoulders tightened.

"No, I just spoke to her yesterday. She, Brad, and the twins are all doing fine." In true Nan fashion, she threw an extra dollop of happy onto her last phrase, as if that were all it took to rewrite history. "You know my little piano student I brag to you about all the time—Savannah?"

"Yeah, sure." My mini panic attack subsided. I clicked on another picture of a Hawaiian bungalow wrapped in the warm glow of a setting sun.

"She was just diagnosed with leukemia."

I stopped clicking. "Oh, Nan. That's awful. How old is she again?"

"Only five. And her mother is a widow—I've grown very close to them."

"Is there anything I can do?"

"Well, yes, actually . . . I was hoping you'd ask." Her voice climbed twelve stories. "I need you to come home for the holidays."

And I fell twelve stories. An image hit my mental screen. Me, in my Hello-Kitty jammies, splayed on a busy sidewalk, broken and bloody.

"*What?* What are you talking about, Nan? I've already booked our vacation."

"I am coordinating a holiday fundraiser for Savannah's medical bills."

I pinched my eyes shut and tried to ignore the tantalizing sound of crashing waves that seemed to lap against my eardrums in perfect time with my pulse. A part of me wanted to throw a tantrum—as fading images of tiki torches and spit-roasted pigs danced across my vision—but who could dismiss a child with cancer?

Scrooge, maybe. But not me.

"But, Nan . . . I really miss you." The emotion inside my throat threatened to unclog.

"And that is precisely why you are going to come to *me* this year. I've worked out everything."

"Does *everything* include a place for me to sleep?"

"Eddy will help me fix up your old room."

"You mean the world's smallest library?"

Nan had turned my old closet of a bedroom into a storage space for all her books after I moved to California. I'd seen some pictures. If Eddy and Nan managed to organize the toppling stacks around the bed, the feat was nothing short of miraculous.

"Now, don't you get sassy with me, Little Miss Hollywood. Your homecoming will be perfect. And it would be the best Christmas present you could give your old granny."

"First of all, no one would dare call you old—at least not to your face. And second, you don't believe in Christmas gifts."

"Say you'll come home, Georgia. *Please.* You never know when it could be my last year."

The dying granny card has officially been played.

"Oh, Nan. Stop it. You're probably in better health than I am." The only good thing in Lenox, Oregon, was my Nan, and I could have her anyplace else. The list of pros and cons knocking against my skull was ten miles long. "Maybe . . . um, I could . . ." *Fly her to LA in the spring?*

Nan let out a squeal, as if my incomplete answer had timed-out. I felt like a contestant on *Jeopardy!* who got buzzed. "Ooh, I'm so excited! We'll have so much fun together. Why don't you head up for Thanksgiving and just stay on through Christmas."

"Wait, I didn't say—"

"Perfect, perfect, perfect. Everyone will be thrilled you're coming home. It's been, what? Seven years? It's time I get to show off my celebrity granddaughter. I'm putting you on the calendar now. In red Sharpie."

"Nan—"

"I just got off the phone with Savannah's mom. I told her I could get you here."

My chest felt like Nan's pressure cooker about to explode. I slumped against the back of my chair.

"You did say you wanted to help Savannah, right?"

My patience was a thin wire—one on which Nan was turning pirouettes like an overeager ballerina. "Why do I need to be in Lenox to help a little girl with cancer?"

"Because I put you in charge of our biggest fund-raiser. The Christmas pageant. Now, I gotta run, darlin'. See you in a few weeks!" The screen on my phone went black.

Face in palm, I sighed the sigh synonymous with defeat. I'd just been bamboozled by my seventy-year-old Nan.

‿

4

Two days before Thanksgiving I loaded up my convertible. My roommate and best friend, Cara, stood in her yoga wear watching me drag a giant suitcase down the stairs of our apartment building. Some best friend she was at zero dark thirty.

"You'll really be gone a month?"

I squinted in the dim light of the parking lot. "Yes, and thank *you* so much for helping me."

My suitcase refused to be squished into the trunk with the other bags so I shoved it into the backseat. Cara walked around to the driver's side door and rubbed her arms with her perfectly manicured hands.

"It's so chilly this morning."

"Cara, it's sixty-four degrees. It is *not* cold."

"Well, it's cold to me. I didn't grow up in some lumberjack town in the hills of Oregon."

"You mean mountains." It was a discussion we'd had at least a dozen times.

"Same thing." She gripped my shoulders with her bony fingers. "Now, give me a hug. I'm gonna miss you!"

Hugging Cara was like embracing a fence post. She was tiny but solid. Owning a popular yoga studio does that to a body—or at least that's what I imagined it does to a body. I had no personal experience.

Planting myself into the front seat, I plugged in my iPhone and scrolled through my apps. It was going to be a very long thirteen hours.

"Maybe you'll meet some hot guy while you're home."

"There hasn't been a hot guy in Lenox since—" I snapped my lips shut. No, I wouldn't think of *him*. "Well, it's been a long time."

Cara whipped her silky blond ponytail over her right shoulder, a mischievous gleam flickering in her eyes. "A lot could have changed."

"Not nearly enough. Love you."

"Love you, too. Drive safe!"

I pulled out of the apartment complex a minute later and headed for the closest coffee drive-thru. Since it was LA, that meant the next corner. *Someone really ought to invent the gallon-size insulated travel mug.* I had checked the weather multiple times over the last few days. Even though the forecast still called for clear skies, I couldn't shake the unsettled nerves in my gut when I thought of driving over the pass. The roads could still be icy.

How had I let Nan talk me into this trip? For the millionth time that morning, I thought about the sunsets, sandals, and surf that I was trading in for slush, snow, and scarves. I picked up my phone and tapped the "Play" icon on my screen.

At least Mary Higgins Clark would keep me company on my long trip home.

℘

I hoped that if I kept my stops to a minimum, I could get over the pass before nightfall. But as the sun dipped below the horizon, I rounded yet another slushy corner. Over the next ten miles, the thermometer in my car alerted me to temperature drops. The wind chill hovered just below freezing.

Nan's house was still an hour or so away. I yawned and cracked the window, and a blast of frigid air raked icy fingers through my hair.

I focused on a blinking sign up ahead.

It read "Chains Required from This Point On."

My stomach scraped against the floorboards. "No, no, no!"

I had chains with me for emergencies, but putting them on after sunset when I hadn't messed with them in almost seven years was not going to be fun.

Pulling off to the side of the road and switching my hazard lights on, I took a shaky breath. *Hello, roadside nightmare. Nice to meet you.*

And in this nightmare two things would happen before I wrangled the chains onto my tires: one, frostbite, and two, hypothermia. The order was irrelevant.

I trudged through the dirty slush to my trunk, pushed several pieces of luggage around, grabbed the clunky chain bag. I felt like I was playing some sort of twisted real-life game of Tetris. I finally located the bag and gave a hearty tug on the handle, only it snagged on a suitcase. I tugged hard—hard—harder. And with one final yank, I was catapulted to the soggy ground. Dirty, slushy snow soaked into the seat of my jeans quicker than I could curse.

I stood and kicked the chain bag toward a tire. Headlights illuminated the paved shoulder, blinding me. I couldn't see the car or the driver. Shading my eyes with my forearm, I imagined that I was in one of those gruesome horror movies: deserted highways, masked men, chainsaws. *Is this going to be my end, God? Really? I would have liked something a bit more original.*

"You need help?"

He didn't sound like a murderer, but what did I know?

"Um . . ."

Mary Higgins Clark would know what to do. Although *my* reaction time mimicked that of a blind tortoise.

"You need help with your chains?" The stranger's voice was deep. Not danger-deep. Dreamy-deep.

I backed up, bumping against my open trunk, wondering what I could grab to use as a weapon if needed. Of course, being able to *see* my murderer would be priority numero uno.

"I, uh . . ."

He was getting closer. I dropped my arm and reached into the trunk behind me and came up with a half-eaten canister of Pringles. *Crapola!*

As it turned out, I needed way more protection than a can of chips.

I knew him. A face from my past.

One . . . two . . . five seconds of shock invaded the space between us.

"Weston James." I spoke his name the way one would spit out a sip of curdled milk.

It was him—only he wasn't the boy I had left behind.

No, this was Weston James, the *man*. And unfortunately time had been good to him. *Too good.*

"Well, well, well. If it isn't Miss Georgia Cole, the Christmas Prodigy herself. I wondered if the rumor I'd heard about you coming back was true."

"Funny, I haven't wondered a *thing* about you." The lie slid over my lips like butter melting on a hill of steaming mashed potatoes.

We stood there—me and the Lenox Heartbreaker—sizing each other up. This was *us*. And it had been us since that fateful day in first grade when he chased me around my desk with a glue stick and threatened to paste my eyelids closed.

He crossed his arms over his well-built chest. My adrenaline spiked, tiny tremors surging through my body. I had to tell myself to shift my gaze to the ground, or the trunk, or the—

"We gonna put those chains on before it gets pitch-black out here, or were you planning to sleep on the highway tonight?"

"I'm sure you'd have no problem leaving me out here."

He smiled a don't-tempt-me smile. Seven years may have passed, but we still had a lifetime of contention to wade through. He bent down, grabbed the chains, and strode past me. His leather jacket pulled tight across his broad shoulders, his dark hair peeked under the sides of his knit cap, and a day's worth of scruff lined his jawbone. I suddenly felt way too hot for the cold night air. I wanted to jump down a giant hole of denial. And stay there.

Laying both chains out ahead of my two front tires, he hopped in the front seat of my car—without asking—started the ignition, and accelerated carefully until the chains were perfectly lined up.

"You can fasten that one." He gestured to the far tire and shut the driver's side door. "Or is that too much to ask of a Hollywood celebrity?"

"Have you ever known me to wimp out?"

I squatted in front of the tire, but that darn chain slipped through my trembling fingers over and over. Weston finished his tire, stretched his arms out like an Olympic swimmer, and sauntered toward me. *Show-off.*

A slight nudge to my left leg by Mr. Roadside Assistance was all it took to knock me over, plunging my backside onto the wet ground once again. "Hey!"

"What?" The sparkle in his eyes matched the wicked grin spreading across his face. "You already looked like you peed your pants. No harm done."

He reached his hand down for me. I swatted it aside. "I guess one doesn't outgrow being *childish*, huh, Wes?"

He knelt and slipped the chain around my tire in ten seconds flat. My teeth chattered through a new wave of shivers. The arctic air threatened to turn me into a living ice sculpture.

Standing again, he took off his jacket and wrapped the warm piece of Weston-smelling leather around my shoulders. "I guess one doesn't outgrow being *obstinate*, huh, Georgia?"

I shrugged off the jacket and tossed it back to him, then opened my car door. I resisted spewing the rebuttals crowding my mind. I needed to save some of them for later. But hopefully, he was just here for Thanksgiving weekend and there wouldn't be a later. I couldn't imagine enduring his smirk for all of December.

I flicked my wrist in his direction, offering him a halfhearted wave. "Thanks for the help—I'm good now."

I slid into my seat and slammed my door, waiting for him to pull out in front of me. It didn't happen. I rolled my window down and waved him on, but still he refused to budge.

Whatever.

For the next hour and ten minutes, Weston James drove behind me on the dark, snowy highway. All the way to Nan's cottage.

As I stepped out of my convertible onto her driveway, he leaned out his window. "See ya around, Sugar Plum Fairy."

Bulging muscles or not, Weston James would always be the annoying little boy with the glue stick—the one I could not seem to erase from my memory.

CHAPTER TWO

"Y ou planning on sleeping all day, Georgia?"
The door creaked open, and Nan's slippers shuffled across
the old wooden floorboards. Turning my head slightly in her direction, my eyes squinted at the burst of light in the hallway behind her.
Though we'd chatted late into the night, I could never sleep past—

"It's seven thirty," Nan said, reading my mind. She had this
creepy ESP thing with me. I never got used to it, especially because
it only worked one way.

I groaned. "Nan, you realize we didn't go to bed till after one,
right?"

"True, but I know how you like to get an early start."

I let my head loll to one side and blinked. "Yes, when I'm
working."

"Well, I hate to tell you this, sweetheart, but I signed you up to
help me today."

I glanced up at the smile that could convince a child to give up
her last piece of candy and chuckled. God only knows what Nan
had in store for us. Sitting up, I swung my legs over the edge of the
twin bed and narrowly avoided knocking a stack of books to the

ground. It was hard to believe I'd spent my childhood sleeping in this coffin-like space.

I picked up the cookbook on top of the pile closest to me, *Best Foods in Brazil.*

"Some great recipes in that one."

I smiled as I flipped through the old, crusty pages that smelled like damp pepper and cloves. That was my Nan. Always trying something new.

"I have some coffee and oatmeal for you on the counter. The senior center needs help preparing for the big day tomorrow. I volunteered us for the shift at nine. Figured you'd want to shower first."

I stretched my arms, yawning as I stood. "Yes, a shower would be good."

She patted my messy hair. "It's so good to have you home."

As her eyes sparkled with tears, a familiar warmth wove through my ribs and cinched my heart. *Home.* "I've missed you too, Nan."

She pulled me close for a hug, one full of the soft, squishy comfort I'd never find in LA.

"Ready to open a few dozen cans of cranberry sauce?"

I clasped my hands together. "It's like my Thanksgiving dream come true."

She swatted my backside. "Go eat your breakfast before it gets cold, smarty-pants."

❧

Nan wasn't kidding.

By the fifteenth can of green beans, I started worrying about carpal tunnel syndrome. The nauseating aroma of soggy vegetables had started to seep into my pores. I shook the stiffness out of my hand and concentrated on breathing through my mouth. Just then, Eddy, wearing her signature navy-blue trench coat, flew through the front door like a bat bolting out of a dark cave. *Some things never change.*

"Georgia Cole! Get your behind over here, and give me a smooch!"

I laughed and wiped my hands on the towel in front of me. "Hi, Eddy."

"You should have heard your grandma talking about you all over town these last few weeks. It was startin' to get on my nerves, and I'm sure I'm not the only one." She kissed my cheek, surely leaving behind her bright-coral lip mark as a souvenir. "Of course, I've never seen her so happy."

"Well, I'm glad I could make her happy." *Even though I should be planning our snorkeling excursion in Hawaii right about now.*

"Wow," she said, taking me in. "You sure are a pretty thing. Look just like your mama did at that age."

I managed a smile, though the compliment fell flat more than it flattered.

"Eddy, give the girl some space to breathe. I don't need you suffocating her on her first day back."

Eddy ignored Nan and pulled up a stool near the counter where I was working. Apparently, she was sticking around. She plucked a green bean out of the pan and smacked on it loudly.

"So, what do you think of the place? Nan give you a tour yet?"

I looked around the senior center—at least what I could see of it from the kitchen. It was a great little space. Cozy and cheery. A perfect spot to socialize: eat, play games, celebrate, and laugh. I was grateful that Nan had it, along with good friends to fill it with.

I nodded. "It's very nice."

"Except for that hideous puke-colored wall over there. Nan insisted on a shade of baby poop."

Nan flung a dish towel at Eddy. "It's *mustard*! And it looks great, I found it in a décor magazine from France."

"Well, maybe the French like staring at bug guts, but I don't." I laughed. Being with these two felt like old habit.

Their comfortable banter reminded me of—*Don't go there, Georgia.*

"What day do you start working with the kids?" Eddy asked.

Confusion plucked me out of reminiscing time. "What kids?"

"The high school kids. They're already rehearsing, you know. Betty's been plunking away on that wretched piano, teaching them Christmas carols down at the church. They're waiting for you." She swung her dirty boot across her knee, holding it in place with her hand. "Looks like that old theater will finally have a purpose again now that you're back. I don't think those doors have been opened in years."

I shifted my eyes to Nan, who was suddenly very busy mixing a bowl of Stove Top stuffing—and humming. "Nan?"

The humming grew louder.

"You're butchering that song, Nan," Eddy said, plugging her ears. "And I don't even care for music all that much."

Nan dropped her spoon into the metal bowl with a clang. "There's a meeting on Saturday to discuss the Christmas pageant. They expect you to be there, Georgia. Everyone's excited about having the 'Holiday Goddess' in town." She beamed, proud of herself for remembering the quote from the article in *USA Today.*

"Nan, please don't call me that. And, like I've told you a thousand times before, writing scripts and directing a production are two very different things. I'll gladly assist in whatever way I can, but I'm sure there's someone else who—"

"There *is* no one else," the women said in unison.

I rolled my eyes and stuck my spoon into a large vat of vanilla custard.

As I brought it to my lips, Nan said, "Just wait till you meet Savannah. She's worth whatever effort you put into this. I promise. You're doing it for her."

Sugar sweetened my tongue while bitterness soured my gut.

&

As I was searching through Nan's overstuffed hall closet for a clean towel, something hard and heavy fell from a shelf. A pink ceramic heart skittered across the old hardwood. I picked it up and cradled it in my hand, clearing away a layer of dust and grime with the tip of my finger. I swallowed the ageless hurt that bubbled up in my throat.

I could easily picture my sixth-grade art class where I'd painted the heart for my mother's birthday. And yet, here it was. Forgotten. Left behind.

I heard her words again, hovering like a haunted memory. *"Don't be like me, Georgia. Go somewhere. Be somebody. Leave this town and never look back."*

Through all the different retellings of the story about the drunken night I was conceived, or the gory details surrounding my birth just days after her seventeenth birthday, my mother's message to me remained crystal clear. It never faltered. No matter how old I became. No matter what goals I achieved.

In fact, she liked the mantra so much that she followed her own advice the spring before my sophomore year in high school.

Move to Florida—*Check.*

Get married—*Check.*

And never look back—*Check.*

I slid down the wall and pulled my knees to my chin. The smell of musty sweaters and blankets lingered in the air around me.

Even when her home address had read Lenox, Oregon, there was always something about my mother that was never truly *home*. Not really. Not with me.

I wasn't surprised when her new marriage took priority.

I wasn't surprised when the birth of her twins filled her days.

I wasn't even surprised when the long silences that spanned three thousand miles and stretched across a dozen states became the rule, not the exception.

But I was surprised by all the *happiness* this new life had brought her.

It was as if the years we'd spent together crammed into Nan's tiny cottage were only the dress rehearsal. And finally, my mother was living her real life.

With a *real* husband and *real* children.

My unplanned birth had stolen her youth, her dreams, her freedom. And though Nan had always been the one to check up on me, tuck me in at night, and kiss my tears away, Summer Cole—my mother—was still the whisper that echoed in my soul.

"Make my sacrifice worth something, Georgia."

∾

"Pass the rice, please!" Eddy shouted at Franklin, her husband. Apparently, in addition to losing his memory, his hearing was also on the fritz. It seemed likely it was related to Eddy's always speaking at a shrill, glass-breaking volume.

It was no surprise that she still held the throne as Lenox's top bingo caller.

A large bowl of rice was passed around the table by Nan's friends, all of them three times my age. I carried Nan's Thanksgiving platter of spicy chicken masala to the table. And no one said a negative word about it. In this crowd, her unconventional ways were accepted—even appreciated. Her friends would eat here before heading over to the center at five for their traditional meal. They had the best of both worlds.

"I saw that Hallmark movie you made," a woman named Pearl with a beak-like nose and tight poodle curls said. "The one about the couple who met on a skating rink, with the guy who had a prosthetic foot."

"Leg," I corrected.

"Yeah, that was a good one. I loved her family—and that Christmas Eve scene—I blubbered like an old fool."

"Thank you, but I just wrote the screenplay. I didn't actually make the movie."

Pearl stared at me blankly. "I just wonder how you write all those things."

I opened my mouth to answer my most asked interview question, *"How do you come up with so many good Christmas stories?"* But as it turned out, that was not what Pearl was asking.

"I mean, all that holiday love and romance stuff. Nan tells us you never go out on dates, so how can you write about something you don't know?"

I choked on an ice cube, and Eddy slammed my back—repeatedly.

Everyone waited for my reply, even Nan. What was this? An intervention for my pathetic love life?

I lifted my chin and met the eyes of each of Nan's guests. "Ever heard of Jane Austen?"

Eddy leaned toward me, eyebrows drawn so tightly it would take pliers to separate them. "You do realize that things didn't turn out quite so well for her in that department, right?"

Okay, fine. Bad example.

Pearl piped up, "Well, there's an eligible bachelor in Lenox that you—"

"More chapati bread, anyone?" Nan asked, standing abruptly.

Thank you, Nan. I owe you one.

Though I smiled at her, her gaze never met mine as she passed the bread basket to her right.

And knowing her like I did, I could tell she was up to something.

CHAPTER THREE

Begrudgingly, I grabbed my satchel off the chair and shoved my laptop inside it. Though the ground was still covered with dirty slush from last week's snowfall, the sun was shining brightly. The temperature was a balmy forty-four degrees. But I needed to walk. Clear my head. Prepare for whatever awaited me at the community theater.

Wrapping a scarf I'd borrowed from Nan's stash around my neck, I stuffed my bare hands into my pockets and made yet another mental note to buy gloves.

My dark chestnut-colored hair flew around my face in the chilly breeze. I was *so* not in California anymore.

Walking past Jonny's Pizza and Gigi's Grocery, I headed north on Main Street. The thick green pine trees lining the streets were a stark contrast to the white-capped mountains in the background. One thing that Lenox had going for it was the scenery that surrounded the town. It was so different from the cement that suffocated LA.

The mountains stirred an emotion in me, making me want to reach for something unseen. I took a deep breath, savoring the feel of clean air in my lungs. I supposed some people felt this way about the ocean, but though the ocean was vast, the mountains were strong and unyielding.

"Georgia?"

I whirled around.

"Wow . . . it *is* you. I heard you were in town."

Sydney Parker stood next to her white SUV and took in every last detail of my wardrobe, stopping on Nan's ratty, rainbow-colored scarf.

"Hello, Sydney, how are you?"

With a tiny lift of her shoulder, she bobbed her head in a way that made her golden locks swish around her shoulders as though she were in a shampoo commercial. "Great. You still single?"

What kind of a question is that?

"Um . . . well, yes . . . actually, I'm—"

"I'm recently divorced. My ex-husband is the mayor," she said as if I'd missed a presidential election. "I live over in Greenway."

Of course, she did. Greenway was the richest neighborhood Lenox had to offer.

"Oh, that's great." *Just keep smiling,* I chided myself. My true feelings have always been hard for me to conceal—or so I've been told.

Sydney Parker's persona in high school screamed *status, status, status.* She befriended the "populars," dated the "populars," and was herself a "popular." We couldn't have been more different back then. And something told me not much had changed.

"You here visiting your grandma?"

"Yeah, and I'm helping out a bit at the theater, too, it seems."

Her face beamed, apparently tapping into a new fuel source that caused her eyes to glow with radioactive freakishness. Then I realized what I had said. My cheeks flamed.

Please don't.

Her high-pitched cackle exploded through the street. "You remember the Christmas play our senior year—"

I shook my head. "Actually, I need to get going. It was nice seeing you, Sydney." *About as nice as stepping into a den of rattlesnakes.*

I hurried down the street, pulling the scarf tighter around my neck to ward off the cold. By the time I made it to the theater for the meeting, I could no longer feel my face. Walking through the small lobby, I heard the laughter of children and the murmur of adult conversation. I hoped to slip into the back and listen to whatever presentation was about to be given, but unfortunately, the second I stepped into the room, applause broke out.

The large crowd parted as Betty Graham grabbed the microphone onstage and waved me forward.

"Everyone, this is Georgia Cole, our town's very own Hollywood celebrity. She's written dozens of Christmas plays, pageants, and even screenplays that have made it onto TV. We are very privileged to have her help us with this charity performance to raise money for Savannah Hart."

The crowd clapped again as she held the microphone out to me.

I stepped forward, and with each stride, I could feel Nan's scarf tightening around my neck like a boa constrictor. My heart pounded against my rib cage as I flipped through a Rolodex of exit strategies in my mind, some more dramatic than others.

I didn't like to speak on stage. I *hated* speaking on stage.

Leaning over to Betty, I whispered, "I'm not sure what you want me to say."

She smiled sweetly, taking my hand as I stopped at the top of the stairs, just shy of the stage. "Just tell us what you'd like us to do, dear. We're ready."

"Ready? *For what?*" My breathy rush of words was hardly audible as I desperately tried to block out the staring eyes around me.

"For the plan. For you to direct us, dear."

Betty pushed the microphone into my sweaty palm. And then it dawned on me. Nan had been serious. There really was no one else.

I scanned the crowd and told myself to say something. To say *anything*. But my pulse was pounding so loudly against my eardrums that I couldn't think, much less speak.

I closed my eyes.

Breathe. Just breathe. I'm twenty-five. This isn't high school.

I held the cool metal to my chin. "Hi . . . I'm Georgia."

Betty nodded at me, her face filled with confusion and maybe even pity. I couldn't be sure.

"I—I'm happy to help. I'll just need some . . . volunteers." After three attempts, I finally swallowed.

"Tell us what you need!" a friendly voice called out.

I swayed and tugged on my scarf as my knees locked in place.

Is it getting dark in here? And why is it four hundred degrees?

Just as my vision spotted and tunneled, a heavy arm wrapped around my shoulders, rocking me back on my heels. As I finally sucked in a breath with enough force to fracture a rib, I saw him. My vision miraculously cleared.

Weston.

"She'll need costume designers, an audio tech, a lighting and stage crew, a musician . . ." Weston rambled on, my mind jolting awake as if I'd been slapped in the face. I tried to shrug off his heavy arm—twice—but his grip held like duct tape.

Betty took the microphone from Weston. "You heard him. Now, who are our volunteers?"

Several ladies toward the front offered to help with costumes and makeup, a nerdy-looking man with glasses said he could run the tech booth and coordinate a lighting crew, and Betty announced that she had the music covered. A large group of older high school students agreed to be the stagehands. That just left—

"We need a set designer," I whispered to Betty.

"I've got the set handled," Weston said with a squeeze.

"That's perfect. Now, what day would you like to officially start rehearsal, Georgia?"

Betty had asked a question, at least I was pretty sure she had, but my thoughts were still on the man plastered to my left side. A waft of sawdust filled my nostrils with every inhalation. *What did she ask me?*

"Georgia?"

I shook my head. "Um . . . Monday evening?"

I elbowed Weston in the ribs, forcing him to release me. He chuckled as I gave him a stare that said, "Don't even think about touching me again."

"Okay, well you heard the lady, folks. We'll start casting Monday night. That leaves us twenty-nine days before production. Susan, can you make sure you send out a town e-mail and get it out on the bulletin boards?"

A lady toward the back shouted, "Sure thing! Thanks again, Georgia."

And just like that, I was officially done with my vacation from Christmas and thrown back into the land of red and green.

After I'd endured several rounds of back pats and cheek pinches, the crowd began to dissipate. Weston dropped to the edge of the stage and swung his legs like a toddler. But *my* legs were still like rubber, so I walked down the steps slowly, trying to process what had just happened.

I was not *normally* prone to panic. Normally, I was confident, self-assured, and levelheaded. But having an entire town depending on me to raise funds for a child with cancer was *not* normal.

"You ready for this, Holiday Barbie?"

I snapped to attention. "It's Holiday Goddess."

His shocking-green eyes traveled the length of my figure shamelessly, his lips in a boyish grin. My scalp tingled when his gaze locked on mine.

I blinked first, breaking the spell. "What are you doing here, Weston? Shouldn't you be traipsing back to Boston? The weekend's almost over."

His eyes lit up with amusement. "You think I live in Boston?"

"Don't you?"

"I—"

"Uncle Wes!" A little girl with blond pigtails skipped over to us, hooking her arms around Weston's legs. Looking away from them, I saw a woman headed our way.

"Willa James?"

"Hi, Georgia. It's good to see you again. And it's actually Willa Hart now." Her smile fought to reach her eyes, failing miserably. But still she hugged me, her touch as soft as a feather.

Willa was Weston's older sister, a girl I'd idolized when I was young. She had everything: beauty, charm, and class. But she was too sweet to envy and too kind to dislike. How she ended up with a brother like Weston was beyond me. Perhaps their parents spent all their good genes on her.

"Is Nan your grandma?" the little girl asked me.

"Yes, she is. And who are you?"

The little girl smiled brightly and held out her hand. "I'm Savannah Hart."

✑

"Why didn't you tell me?" Hands on my hips, I scowled at Nan.

"Tell you what, dear?" Nan peeked over her glasses as she worked her daily crossword puzzle.

Tossing my satchel onto a chair, I sighed. "You know exactly what I'm talking about. Weston James is Savannah's uncle?"

Nan lifted her head, her eyes bright with feigned innocence. "Well, Georgia, you trained me a long time ago to stop updating you on Weston. Every time I so much as mentioned his name, you'd cut me off—tell me you didn't want to hear about him or his endeavors. So if you failed to make that particular connection until today, the only person to blame is yourself. I would have gladly volunteered that information if only you would have asked."

I swear, if she weren't seventy I'd—

"Weston James is a *good* man, Georgia—one of the best men I know. He's taken care of—"

"Weston James is a competitive jerk. I know him *very* well, Nan." *Even if he is the most attractive jerk in the history of humankind.*

She took her glasses off and laid them beside her on the table. "You sure that's how you should feel about him now, after all these years? Don't you think people can change?"

"Not him—no. And thanks to you, I'm stuck working next to him for the next four weeks."

I flung myself onto the sofa, realizing how childish I sounded, especially in comparison to what a certain five-year-old girl was about to face. "I'm sorry . . . I do want to help Savannah. She seems like a really special little girl."

"She is . . . In fact, she reminds me of someone else I know."

"Who?"

"You, darlin'. She's kindhearted, funny, and one of the most determined people I've ever known. She *will* beat this cancer. We just need to help her do it."

I leaned my head against a couch pillow and closed my eyes.

What pageant have I written that I can throw together in only four weeks?

It was going to be a very long holiday season.

❧

I sat on the floor next to the fireplace with a dozen papers scattered on the floor beside me. Hair up and yoga pants on, I hunkered down for a long night of note-taking and scene revisions. Though it wasn't what I'd consider my best work, I chose a play that was fairly consistent with the Christmas story itself. I suspected that was what the town of Lenox would appreciate most. And since I didn't have a lot of time or resources to work with, it would have to do.

When Nan had requested my presence at church that morning, I simply held up my notebook paper and Post-it Notes, and she went on her way without another word. *The woman couldn't get everything she wanted, right?*

❧

Nan was working on her fund-raising plans at the kitchen table while classical jazz played somewhere in the background. *No Christmas music.* That had been my only request. She must have been feeling generous because she honored it—no questions asked. As I made a note about lighting, I pictured the beautiful blond child I met yesterday at the theater. I couldn't get her face, her smile, her *joy* out of my mind.

My chest warmed when I thought about the way she tapped each of Weston's fists, knowing there was a piece of gum waiting for her inside one. She chose correctly. Everything about her seemed healthy and whole. It was nearly impossible to believe that something so toxic lived inside her.

A loud rap on the door caused me to drop my pen.

"I'll get it," Nan practically sang.

I expected Eddy's shrill bark to reverberate off the walls any second, but instead, I heard a familiar baritone.

"Good evening, Nan."

I froze. *Why is he here?*

"Is Georgia around?"

"She sure is . . . right over there, roasting herself by the fireplace."

I pretended not to hear the conversation that was just twenty feet from me and began writing completely illegible notes on the paper next to my thigh.

"Hey."

A knot formed at the base of my belly when I glanced up at him. The scent of freshly cut timber lingered between us. And though my pulse quickened to a staccato, I replied as coolly as possible, "Hey."

"I was asked to give you something." He pulled an envelope from the back pocket of his jeans.

"Please have a seat, Weston. Can I get you a cup of coffee or hot chocolate?" Nan asked from the kitchen.

Really, the woman was nearly insufferable at times. I hid my inner eye roll.

"Oh, well . . . if it isn't any trouble. A cup of coffee would be great. Black, please."

"Decaf?"

"Nah, I'll be up for a while tonight."

Weston took a seat across from me on the floral sofa. *What is happening here?* I touched the messy bun atop my head in search of stray locks, suddenly self-conscious as his gaze fixated on my face.

I looked down at the envelope in my hands and ran a finger under the flap on the back.

"It's from Savannah," Weston said.

I pulled out two folded pieces of construction paper and studied them both silently. The first was a letter, addressed to me in the sweetest—and messiest—handwriting I'd ever seen.

Dear Miss Georgia,
Thank you for helping me. I love when the angel comes to Mary. I
want to see an angel someday.
Love,
Savannah

On the second page was a picture of Savannah's angel with Mary. She labeled them both. And the best part was that Mary looked to be in jeans and a T-shirt. I smiled at her originality.

"I think that's the first honest smile I've seen since you got here."

I wiped it from my face immediately.

Tucking the paper back inside the envelope, I forced out a reply: "Please tell her I said thank you."

"She's leaving in the morning for Portland—to start her treatments."

My gut twisted and my gaze flickered to his briefly. "I'm sorry."

Biting my bottom lip, I stared at the papers scattered around me.

There were several seconds of uncomfortable quiet, the kind that made my skin itch. I swallowed. Finally, Nan strolled in with Weston's coffee. She handed him the mug.

"I think I'll head back to my bedroom to read. Gotta keep the old mind in shape. Good night, kids."

Naturally.

Weston said good night to her, and I imagined all the ways I could drain his coffee mug so that he would make a quick exit as well.

"So . . . what are you doing down there on the floor?" he asked.

"Working."

He chuckled. "Anything I can help you with?"

You leaving would help me immensely. "Nope. I've got it covered," I said, marking page numbers on the script in front of me.

"You haven't changed."

Was that an insult? "Sorry to disappoint."

"Who said I was disappointed?"

My breathing faltered, and I forced my next words to the surface. "Listen, I want to help your niece, Weston. She seems like a great little girl. And you know I'll do my best to raise the funds she needs for her medical care, but I do not have energy to do . . . whatever *this* is." I looked up at him despite my internal protest. "I'll have your scene list ready by tomorrow night so you can build the sets accordingly."

"So, that's it, then?"

I gawked at him. *What else does he want from me?*

"Um . . . pretty much, yeah."

"Fine." He stood, placing his mug on the coffee table beside me.

"Fine," I said, standing quickly to beat him to the front door.

Swinging it wide, I felt a burst of frosty air bite my face and sting my eyes. Weston took two steps out the door, then turned to face me again. My lungs emptied of oxygen as I worked to rip my gaze from his.

"I live in the blue house on Maple and Tenth."

He lives here . . . in Lenox?

I opened my mouth to ask—

"You can take your set demands there after rehearsal tomorrow night."

The wind cut through me, and I shivered. "You're not coming?"

"Are you *asking* me to come?" His eyes sparked with challenge, but I refused the bait. I didn't need him. I would never rely on Weston James.

Not again.

"No."

He chuckled before jogging down the steps toward the walkway. Just as I closed the door, I heard, "Good night, Miss Figgy Pudding."

CHAPTER FOUR

I'd been staring up at the ceiling in my tiny bedroom for hours, thinking about Savannah's letter—and a certain uncle of hers.

Whether it was the seventh-grade home economics bake-off when Weston put cumin in my oatmeal cookies instead of cinnamon, or when I stole his shoelaces before the timed mile run in PE our sophomore year, Weston and I had more stories than a library could contain. Our entire childhood—kindergarten through high school graduation—overflowed with our shared history. He teased me relentlessly growing up, and I had secretly relished his attention.

We ran in completely separate circles, if you could call my complete lack of social status a circle. But even though we were never officially friends, I knew Weston James had accepted me even when none of the others had.

And it was all fun and games until—

I sat up in bed, unwilling to let my mind wander any further. Instead, I fixated on something else entirely. Throwing off my covers, I made a dash for the living room, where I'd left Savannah's letter. I pushed her grateful words aside and lifted the creative drawing of her modern-day Mary to the dying firelight.

Modern Mary.

And that's when I struck gold. At 3:03 on Monday morning. *Why does creativity flourish at the most inopportune times?*

I grabbed my laptop from the sofa and clicked open a new document. Instead of the blink of the cursor taunting me, I found a friendly challenge. A new story waited to be told. Yes, I may have been *so over* Christmas plots in general, but there was something quite enticing about a modern-day Nativity scene. I picked up the pile of scattered papers marked with useless notes and set them aside.

I lifted up a silent prayer, hoping I could pull this off in time for the casting.

And then I typed. Furiously.

Fifteen hours and counting . . .

Sleep was overrated anyway.

❧

With a fresh script in one hand, my fourth cup of double-shot espresso in the other, and my undereye concealer as thick as painter's putty, I was ready to face the music—literally. I could hear the plunking of piano keys from the parking lot.

As the doors of the theater whooshed open, I found myself searching every face. True to his word, Weston wasn't there. I wasn't sure how to feel about that.

I hated the idea of him hovering around, yet driving to his house later to drop off the set plans was likely a worse fate.

Betty took the stage. "Gather around everyone. Our director is here."

I walked toward the stage, quietly refusing to join her up there. Once had been enough. I stayed on the floor just below her. When I reached for the microphone, she looked at me with confusion in her eyes.

"I'm fine down here. Thank you, Betty." She nodded, handing it over immediately.

"Thank you all for coming tonight," I began. "I'll be casting for the roles in *Modern Mary* in a few minutes, but if there isn't a role for you, please know that we can still use you somewhere. This production will take a lot of work to pull off. We may have set a lofty goal, but it's for a good cause. Let's not forget that."

I heard several verbal confirmations before I continued. "This play is a new one." *The I-wrote-it-this-morning kind of new.* "It was actually inspired by Savannah herself, and I hope you'll be as excited as I am about it. It's the Christmas story we all know . . . but set in modern times. What if Mary were a freshman in high school? What if the wise men were stockbrokers from New York? What if the shepherds who were out tending their flocks were actually cowboys on a dude ranch? It's the same story with a modern twist."

"Don't you think it's sacrilegious to make the Virgin Mary a high school student?"

I stood on my tiptoes to see where the sharp voice had come from. It didn't take long to find the source. Sydney Parker stood to the side, arms crossed over her large and perky chest.

"I mean, really? That sounds like a bad holiday TV special."

Her well-planned dig was easy enough to avert.

"Well, good thing it's just a pageant then, one to raise money for a sick little girl who loves to draw Mary in jeans and a T-shirt."

The sour look on Sydney's pouty lips intensified.

"Anyone else?" I asked the crowd.

"Sounds cool!" an older teenage boy yelled. "I've never seen anything like that."

"Yeah. Let's do it!" another one said.

I wiped the smirk meant for Sydney from my face and then announced each part. Audition lines formed as Betty and I settled into the front-row theater seats. I found myself wishing for a third person to help with the judging, dismissing Weston's face as soon as it came to mind. I looked around the crowd again and saw an old acquaintance from high school, Misty Peach.

She was as sweet as her name implied, and better yet, she had been a stagehand for our high school plays. I swallowed the humiliation that surfaced when I thought about one particular production and waved her over. She looked more than a little surprised.

"Hey, Georgia—did you need me?"

"Yes! Hey, Misty." I smiled and touched her shoulder. "Would you mind helping me cast tonight? It's better to have three heads instead of two. That way there's a tiebreaker."

She bit her lip. "Well . . . I suppose I could do that. I'm not very qualified, though, I'm afraid. I'm a stay-at-home mom, not a professional in . . . well, anything."

I squeezed her arm. "You'll be perfect."

"If you say so. I do love Savannah. She's in my son's kindergarten class at school . . . I think this is a great idea."

I patted the chair next to me. "Thank you, Misty."

For the next two hours, I listened, took notes, and tried not to yawn or fall off my seat from exhaustion as every able body in Lenox tried out for *Modern Mary*.

When the last audition was done, my eyes actually started to leak tears—a mixture of fatigue, joy, and pure delirium.

The three of us agreed on every casting decision except for the boy who would play Joseph. Betty was insistent on giving the part to Ben (a teenager who picked his nose halfway through his reading and proceeded to wipe it on his jeans) whereas I felt Justin was a better fit. Thank goodness Misty chimed in with her two cents.

"Betty, Ben may be your nephew, but we can't show favoritism in casting. Justin is my choice, too, and majority rules."

I like this girl.

"Well, it sounds like we're done here, then." I yawned as Betty moved to stand up. "Thank you both for your input tonight. Betty, I'm grateful for your help with the music." Her countenance lifted at the compliment.

"I'm glad to help." She grinned, her short salt-and-pepper hair bouncing with each step as she walked out the door.

"Misty, how would you like to be my assistant?"

She smiled wide. "Really? I'd love to. Thank you, Georgia. I'll just need to work out child care in the evenings with my husband, but it shouldn't be a problem."

I covered a yawn with my fist. "Great, thank you."

She hugged me. "It's so nice to have you home, Georgia."

Home. There was that word again.

❧

As I parked in front of Weston's house, adrenaline surged through my veins.

Unwilling to let my guard down in front of him for a single minute, I reminded myself that this interaction needed to be quick. The less time in Weston's company, the better. I may not have slept for nearly forty hours, but I could surely keep it together for a few more minutes—sleep deprived or not. I blinked my eyes against the stinging cold and tucked the set list under my arm. I rubbed my hands together to create warmth that wasn't there.

Gloves. Why can't I remember to buy some darn gloves?

Walking toward the blue house on the corner of Maple and Tenth, I wondered, not for the first time, why he was living in Lenox . . . not building skyscrapers in Boston.

I knocked, and the door opened.

He stood there, forearm resting against the doorjamb, his gray T-shirt pulled tight across his chest and biceps. My eyes ignoring

34

the warning bells sounding in my head, I took in his low-slung jeans. *Was he for real?* I swallowed hard, trying to will moisture back into my mouth.

"Here." The word escaped like a glorified croak as I tried to hand him the highlighted set list, but he scowled at it as if I'd just pulled the sheaf of paper from a public toilet.

"That's not how I do things."

"What are you talking about?" I asked, shivering.

"If you want me to build a set for you, you can come inside and talk with me about it—civilly."

"No." I crossed my arms, the papers crinkling.

He crossed his, too. "Then you better go down to Ernie's Hardware in the morning and see if he can help you. Oh, and don't worry, I hear he still has one good eye."

Urgh! "You're impossible."

"And you're as irritating as—"

I growled and pushed past him. Surprisingly, his house was quite nice inside. I wouldn't dare compliment him, though. We were *not* friends anymore. We were simply working on a Christmas play together.

I still couldn't quite believe that little twist of irony—which at the moment felt more like a stab wound.

"You can sit down over there. Want a cup of coffee?"

I glanced at the clock and did a quick calculation. *Thirty-nine and a half hours without sleep.* I nodded. Coffee would be necessary for me to make it through even a five-minute conversation. I sat on his leather sofa and took out my phone, texting Nan. *Dropping off set info to Weston. Be home soon.*

An immediate reply: *Going to bed. Don't rush back. :)*

Sinking into the couch, I closed my eyes as I took in a big whiff of masculinity: sawdust, leather, and—

"Georgia?"

I jolted awake, heart galloping.

"Were you just drooling on my couch?"

I wiped my mouth, embarrassed by the moisture left on my hand. "Um . . . I was just admiring your sofa. It's nice . . . for a bachelor, I mean." *Wait, is he a bachelor?*

He placed the coffee mugs on the side table and sat in the recliner next to me. "You interested in my personal life, Georgia?"

"No." The heat creeping up my neck felt like it would set my hair on fire. "Let's just get this over with." I picked up the highlighted script and handed it to him. He began reading it immediately.

"This new?" he asked.

"What?"

"This play. Did you just write this?"

How does he know that?

I shrugged, unwilling to tell him more than he needed to know.

"I haven't seen this one." He flipped through the pages.

What was that supposed to mean?

Something sparked to life around us—something I wanted to pound until it begged for mercy and died a slow and painful death, but my curiosity won out.

"You've seen more than one of my movies?"

"I've kept tabs on you, Georgia Cole." His eyes pierced me through, and I turned my head quickly.

"Well, I can't say I've done the same for you."

"You knew I moved to Boston."

"Everyone knew you were headed there after graduation."

His smile was bold, unyielding. "You're hardly 'everyone.'"

Was he flirting with me? Somehow I didn't think that was possible.

"Why *are* you in Lenox anyway?" I pulled my legs underneath me and anchored my elbow on the arm of the sofa. My head felt like it weighed two hundred pounds, and it was getting heavier by the second.

I knew I was getting off topic, but the fogginess in my brain made it nearly impossible to think clearly.

"I moved back after Chad died."

Leaning my head toward him, I searched his eyes. Such a simple statement, yet I knew it wasn't. Chad Hart was Willa's high school sweetheart. They were newlyweds when I left town for LA. They were also the Barbie and Ken of Lenox—molded to love one another.

It was all coming back now, like an old dusty memory. Nan had called me years ago while I was in college to tell me that Chad had died of an aneurysm. But did I know Willa was pregnant at the time? No. Somehow I hadn't realized that the little girl Nan raved about for the last year was Willa and Chad's daughter.

"You came home . . . for Willa?" A dull ache radiated in my chest.

He nodded, his face solemn, not a trace of humor or amusement to be found.

"And you never went back?"

"I finished up school in Bend, at Central. I teach shop at the high school."

If shock didn't require so much energy, I would have fallen off the sofa. But as it was, Weston's head was starting to blur into multiples.

"You gave up your scholarship? What about architecture?" I asked, yawning. The steam from my coffee cup had stopped billowing minutes ago, and I hadn't taken one sip.

He studied my face, and this time I couldn't break the sleepy trance that washed over me. Or the feeling of calm. My eyelids grew heavy again as my head slid off my hand to rest fully on the padding of my arm.

I felt my hair being brushed away from my face, and then I heard him whisper, "Some things are more important than ambition, Georgia."

CHAPTER FIVE

I snuggled deeper into the blanket and rolled over, savoring the last few moments of sleepy bliss. Something sweet and familiar was in the air. I breathed it in, my stomach growling in response. *Did Nan bake something special for breakfast?*

And then I heard a hum.

But it was *not* a Nan hum.

My eyes snapped open. *Oh my gosh . . . Oh my gosh . . . Oh my gosh.*

The blanket slid to the floor as I assessed my current surroundings, nausea meeting my gut like a head-on collision.

Weston's living room.

Please, oh please, let this be a really bad dream.

"You're awake."

I wiped under my eyes frantically, trying to remove any trace of raccoon-eye smears before working to right my twisted shirt.

"What time is it?"

"You sound like an old man in the morning."

"Morning?" I looked out the window. Sure enough, it was dawn. "How could you let me sleep here?"

A freshly showered Weston sauntered toward me. "Hey, calm down Miss Grinch. It's a little before seven . . . and because friends don't let friends drive asleep. But let me tell you, you were doing a lot more than sleeping. You were snoring and—"

"And you couldn't have just woken me up like a normal person? What is wrong with you?" I yanked the hair tie off my wrist and gathered my matted mane into a ponytail. "Nan is probably worried sick."

"I called her. She's fine."

I snorted at his nonchalant response. *Typical.* Sure, maybe somewhere deep down I could see how this act might seem sweet, or maybe even noble, but not here . . . not with *him.*

My cheeks burned as an unwelcome memory washed over me, his face at the center of it all.

"We're not friends, Weston."

I grabbed my boots, which were propped next to his couch, and as I tugged them on, my body suddenly stiffened. *Had he taken my shoes off? How had I slept that hard?* I pressed my lips together. I knew better than to be vulnerable with him, and falling asleep on his blasted sofa couldn't *be* more vulnerable! I pulled my jacket on and headed toward the door.

"Georgia, stop."

My hand froze on the dead bolt, his voice at my back. I fought against the emotion building in my throat, my heart pounding to the cadence of an old, familiar drum.

"You and I need to have a conversation. One that should have happened seven years ago."

I shook my head adamantly. "No, we don't."

His hand gripped my shoulder. He was so close that his breath tickled my ear. "Then why can't I forget you, Georgia Cole?"

Squeezing my eyes shut, I felt my voice transform into a shaky whisper of doubt. "I don't know . . . but I forgot you."

"Turn around and say that to my face, then." It was a challenge; one I knew I couldn't accept.

My breath stopped as he slid his hand down the length of my arm, causing my traitorous body to melt under his touch.

But the voice inside my head prevailed.

Don't give in.

"What are you so afraid of?"

"Nothing." *You.* "*Please*, just let me leave."

He withdrew his hand and took a step back. I pulled open the door and charged down the front steps two at a time, putting as much distance between us as I possibly could.

"I knew the real you once, Georgia . . . and I'm willing to bet I still do. No matter what you believe, I have *always* been your friend."

As I shut myself inside my car, his words splintered into my soul one after another.

I had spent *years* convincing myself the opposite was true.

That he hadn't accepted me.

That he hadn't understood me.

That he hadn't cared for me.

Because if Weston James had truly known me, then he had *intended* to crush me that December night long ago.

❧

I hear the crowd: the coughs, the laughs, the murmurs. And I feel a momentary buzz of panic wash over me. But I push it down. This is my passion. My dream. My purpose.

I spent the last twelve years making good grades, acing tests, winning awards, all to prove that I could be intelligent and imaginative at the same time. And here I am: the lead in the Christmas play. Me, the girl who played "pretend family" in the park by my house. Me, the girl who read books for fun because mom said having friends would get me in trouble. Me, the girl Weston James walked home yesterday after rehearsal.

My stomach spasms when I remember his words, despite the prompting inside me to guard my heart.

"These last three months have changed something for me, Georgia. I see you . . . differently, or maybe I just finally see what's always been there. I don't know . . . but I don't want to go back to how things were before."

"Five minutes to curtain," someone calls, breaking my trance.

I glance at Weston across the open chasm of stage. He's talking to our drama teacher, Mr. Daniels.

"Georgia," Sydney Parker, my new understudy, says.

"Yeah?"

"Mr. Daniels told me to ask you about a scene change at the end of Act Two. He wants to add the kiss back in to that last scene—it's the way it was originally written, you know."

My eyes widen to the size of grapefruits. "Wh—what are you talking about?"

"Mr. Daniels thought it would add a bit more excitement. He's talking to Weston about it right now, and he asked me to relay the message, see if you're up for it."

Kiss Weston James? The popular, charming, funny, and pursued-by-every-teenage-girl-within-a-hundred-mile-radius Weston James?

I stare across the stage skeptically and see both Weston and Mr. Daniels nodding and smiling in my direction. And when Weston gives me the wink—the one I've seen since our days on the playground, the one that says, "I'm in if you are"—my doubt melts.

And so does the last protective layer surrounding my heart.

I look to Sydney once again. "Okay, tell me exactly what I'm supposed to do."

And she does. In detail.

The blocking. The leap. The passionate lip-lock that is to take place. But when I run toward him, he doesn't look at me with longing and desire. He doesn't grab me around the waist. And he certainly doesn't kiss me with fervent zeal. Instead, he takes a step back, causing me to crash to the floor, rip my dress, and roll off the stage with a painful thud.

I lie in shock, the laughs blurring together as I wallow in my shameful foolishness. But there is one voice I hear clearly through the crowd when the director demands an explanation for the halted show. Sydney Parker's.

She's cozied up to Weston onstage, smiling. "Weston, if you wanted a girl to throw herself at your feet, you should have just asked!"

It's then I realize I've been the butt of Weston's best practical joke yet.

I jump to my feet as the crowd continues to laugh, and I run from the auditorium.

As I weep alone in the same park that at one time housed my imaginary parents, siblings, and friends, I break. Fragments of memories pull at my subconscious and bring the only resolve I can muster: I can't face Weston again. I can't see his eyes, or hear his voice, or continue to believe that our childhood friendship had meant something to him—at least the way it had to me. Whatever game he was playing, I couldn't play it anymore. I had loved him for as long as I could remember, wishing that one day he might return my sentiments.

I'd been a fool.

And I realize with painful clarity that my mom's advice is the only way to mend my broken heart.

The first chance I get, I leave town.

I leave my memories.

And I leave Weston James.

☙

It was just after seven when I pulled up to Nan's. The puff of the chimney told me she was awake. *Awesome. The walk of shame in front of my grandmother.* This day was rapidly going downhill, and I had been awake for less than an hour.

"Good morning!" Nan sang out the second I opened the door. She stood near the kitchen table, drinking her morning cup of coffee, swaying gently in her ratty bathrobe.

I grimaced. "Hi, Nan. I promise you, it's not how it looks. I didn't sleep the night before because I was up writing, and I must have passed out from exhaustion on his couch, and then he didn't—"

"Good grief, girl. You're going to pass out if you keep talking without pausing to breathe. I don't think it looks any which way." She smiled over the top of her mug as I exhaled. "That said, you probably shouldn't go making a habit of falling asleep on every good-looking man's couch."

Something about seeing her calmed me. *My Nan.* My ever-dependable, loving Nan.

"Sit with me, darlin'."

I did as I was told, pulling out a chair at the dining room table and plunking myself into it with a thud. And a sigh.

"What's wrong?" She leaned her elbows on the tabletop.

I started to shake my head, but she covered my hand with hers. It was impossible for me to deny the truth. Who needed a lie detector when the world had Nan?

"I feel like I just took a giant step back in time by coming here. Being in Lenox makes me feel like a stupid high school girl again."

"You are a lot of things, Georgia. But stupid has never been one of them."

I shrugged. "That's debatable."

She chuckled, spinning the mug in her hands. "You and Weston were always the talk of the town. How many times did I have to pick you up from the office after some silly prank? Even as a young boy, he could ruffle your feathers quicker than anyone else."

"Yeah, I know." This was not news to me.

"Don't you ever wonder *why?*"

I stared at her. "I know why, he's just so . . ." *What is he, exactly?*

She raised her eyebrows. "Yes?"

I couldn't possibly sum him up in one word.

Nan laughed hard. "Sweetheart, I think you might be trying to define the wrong thing."

I laid my head on the table in silent surrender.

"I can't be around him, Nan. I just can't." I heard his words in my head again, and my eyes stung. *"I knew the real you once . . . and I'm willing to bet I still do."*

"Georgia, *can't* is a four-letter word in this house. Nothing's ever stopped you before. You're a strong, independent, fearless woman. Whatever happened between you two was seven years ago. Don't you think it's time to move forward? Just because this town may look the same doesn't mean there aren't surprises waiting around every corner. I've lived here all my life, and I uncover something new every single day. Allow yourself to see with fresh eyes, Georgia."

I wasn't sure if she was referencing Lenox or Weston, but in true Nan style, she let me mull it over without further explanation.

⁊

"So . . . you've moved up the ladder to director now? Geesh, who knew visiting Nowheresville, Oregon, could have career benefits?" Cara's playful tone made me smile.

I switched my phone to my right ear as I pulled on my Uggs and jacket. The sun was shining today, but it was still crisp. Regardless of the temperature, I needed the fresh air *and* the stroll. Cara could keep me company on my way to the high school. When Misty, my new assistant director, had called me earlier that morning with a few blocking ideas, I decided I'd better head to town and get the theater key from the school secretary—the same secretary who had both unlocked *and* relocked the door for us last night after auditions. Apparently, there was only *one* key, and Mrs. Harper was its guardian, even though it was technically owned by a real estate broker. I had a feeling I was going to have to sign my life—and future generations' lives—away in order to get it, too.

"It's community theater, Cara, not Broadway. The cast is mostly made up of high school students."

"Ooh . . . like *Glee*? Any hot music teachers?" she asked.

No, only hot shop teachers.

"Not quite. How were your classes today?"

"Great. You'll never believe who signed up. You know that blond from that one movie with the shark in Hawaii . . ."

And with that, Cara was lost in her own little world of Hollywood stardom. The number of actors and actresses who came into her yoga studio was obscene. I laughed at her creative descriptions as I passed the post office and the secondhand bookstore.

". . . and then I was like, 'no bleeping way!' and she was like, 'yes bleeping way'—"

"Hey, Cara—I gotta go. I'll text you tonight, okay?"

"Cool. Just don't die in an avalanche walking to the high school, okay?"

"Cara, you really need to read up on the Northwest, sweetie."

I ended the call and peeked through the large picture window of Sullivan's Bookstore but was surprised to see that old, crotchety Mr. Sullivan was not the one behind the counter. I loved the store, but the foul mood of Mr. Sullivan usually kept me away. On the glass door was a cheery sign that read "Sunshine Books." I smiled, remembering Nan's words to me. *"Allow yourself to see with fresh eyes, Georgia."*

"Good afternoon, may I help you find something?" the woman at the counter asked.

My lips twitched into a grin, and I was momentarily shocked at the difference one attitude can have on an atmosphere. *The knife of Nan's words kept twisting.*

"No, thanks. Just wanted to browse for a few minutes," I said before doing a double take. "Mrs. Brown?"

Her head shot up again from the open book on her lap. "Georgia? Oh, I'm so happy you came in today! I was hoping to run into you."

My high school guidance counselor embraced me so tightly I nearly coughed. "I heard what you're doing for the Harts, and I think it's wonderful."

"When did you buy this store, Mrs. Brown?"

She laughed. "I'm retired now, no need for formalities. Please call me Violet. Let's see . . . It's been about three years ago now."

"Well, it looks great."

We chatted for a few minutes more, catching up on the last seven years, including my notorious Hallmark movies, with which she seemed well acquainted.

As I strolled through the store, touching the spines of dozens of books, I thought of Nan. She had planted a love of reading in me many years ago.

There were so many stories, plots, dreams, and visions enclosed in this tiny space. So many hours of toilsome labor. After browsing through the mystery and romance sections, I came to a small shelf labeled "Classics."

I stopped abruptly.

"No way," I whispered.

I carefully lifted the pale-blue leather-bound copy of *Little Women* from the shelf and found my eyes misting up for a second time that day. This was Nan's favorite book—mine, too. It was the first chapter book she'd ever read to me. It's what inspired me to become such an avid reader and writer. Nan always said that I was her Jo March.

How I had longed for a family like the Marches.

Ironically, I didn't long for a daddy nearly as much as I longed for sisters . . . and for a mom who enjoyed being a mother.

I flipped to the back, reading one of my favorite passages—though I'd almost committed it to memory like so many other passages in this book. Laurie (Teddy), who'd loved Jo as a child, shows up and surprises her by announcing he's married Amy, Jo's sister.

I could almost hear his voice as I read the passage:

"You both got into your right places, and I felt sure that it was well off with the old love before it was on with the new, that I could honestly share my heart between sister Jo and wife Amy, and love them dearly. Will you believe it, and go back to the happy old times when we first knew one another?"

"I'll believe it, with all my heart, but, Teddy, we never can be boy and girl again. The happy old times can't come back, and we mustn't expect it. We are man and woman now, with sober work to do, for playtime is over, and we must give up frolicking."

"I never could get over that ending."

I jumped at the sound of Violet's voice.

Dreamily, I sighed, picturing the scene at the end where Friedrich comes to find Jo and mistakes her as the March sister who has recently married. Jo chases after him in the rain, and he says, "But I have nothing to give you. My hands are empty." Jo intertwines her fingers with his and says, "Not empty now."

"Yes, that's a great scene," I agreed.

"No, it's not. It's torturous!"

I took a step back and turned to face her. "What do you mean?"

"I think Louisa May Alcott got it wrong. I wanted Teddy to marry Jo. They were meant for each other."

I gaped at her bold words. This was pure sacrilege—and in a bookstore no less! I took another step back in case a bolt of lightning came down to strike her where she stood.

"But Teddy *couldn't* marry Jo! There was too much history between them, too many childish memories and—" *Calm down, Georgia.*

Violet beamed. "I can get pretty passionate about books, too. It's why I wanted to buy this place from mean old Mr. Sullivan."

I studied the old leather book in my hand. "How much is this?"

She looked at the book and then back at me. "It was appraised at five hundred. It's a first edition, printed in 1911."

I had spent more than that on Nan for vacations, but a single book for five hundred dollars? Nan would lock me out of the house if she knew I'd spent that kind of cash on a gift. Anyway, she didn't *do* gifts. She believed we should bless one another all year round with acts of service instead of some onetime piece of garbage (her words, not mine). That being said, the woman had more books than anyone I knew—and she cherished them like no one else I knew.

"Okay. I'd like to get it."

Violet's eyebrows shot up as she took the book from me and placed it on the counter. She didn't move as she stared at me. "I'll tell you what . . . I'll give you twenty percent off if you'll come back and tell me all the reasons you think Jo and Teddy weren't right for each other."

My eyes widened. "Really?"

"Yep. I found this at an estate sale and got it for dirt cheap. I'll still be making a profit, I promise you."

I was intrigued. Definitely intrigued.

"Okay. Deal."

"Great. I love a good literary debate—especially over a classic like *Little Women*."

She rang it up and wrapped the book, so I could stick it into my satchel and hide it when I got home.

"Thank you, Violet."

"You're welcome. Now, don't forget to stop by, okay?"

I nodded as the bells on the door announced my departure.

CHAPTER SIX

Just as I predicted, Mrs. Harper lectured me quite extensively before handing over the theater key. I wanted to fire back with a little speech of my own, starting with, "Listen, lady, I didn't ask to direct a Christmas play during my vacation," and ending with, "Perhaps you should go make a few copies down at Ernie's Hardware if you're that concerned about losing the key." But I simply smiled and kept my mouth shut.

As I walked out of the school office and slipped the treasured key into my coat pocket, a throat cleared behind me. I knew before turning around exactly whom that throat belonged to.

"You just can't stay away from me, can you?"

"I actually forgot you worked here." Big. Fat. Lie.

Weston's eyes may have reflected disbelief, but he didn't call me out. Instead, he said, "Do you have a minute? I need to show you something . . . in the shop."

I glanced around. No students. Deserted hallway. *Didn't anyone hang around after dismissal anymore?*

After our awkwardly intimate exchange this morning, it seemed strange to debate such a small request, but that was exactly what I was doing. The school held a lethal number of memories, especially where Weston was concerned.

"I can spare five minutes," I lied again. In fact, I had over an hour before I was supposed to meet Misty at the theater.

Weston strode down the long hallway. Apparently, I was supposed to follow him.

The large shop had a concrete floor and was filled with workbenches, saws of many varieties, and wood. Lots of wood. I realized why Weston always smelled like freshly cut timber.

I touched one of the tall countertops and swiped my finger through a fine layer of dust.

"Bring back memories?"

I glanced up at Weston, who was studying me from across the room. I took in his dark wash jeans and olive thermal shirt. My cheeks burned with awareness. He wasn't like any high school teacher I remembered. That was for sure. And I was willing to bet he had quite a large group of cougar moms following him around—not the kind with fur and fangs. Okay, perhaps fangs.

"Not all memories should be resurrected," I mumbled under my breath.

He slapped a large piece of graph paper onto the counter and pulled up a metal stool beside me. I remained standing.

Resting his chin on his palm, he said, "I don't know. I can recall some pretty good ones. Remember our build-off junior year?"

"You mean the one where you paid Jimmy Lawkins to spray paint all my tools pink?"

"Well, it's not like you didn't retaliate."

I laughed easily, remembering how I'd managed to steal his remaining allotted nails, which ultimately helped me win the competition.

"A woman must never reveal her secrets."

He grinned his wickedly annoying smile, dimples grooving deep, while my stomach plummeted fifty floors.

Needing a quick diversion, I refocused my attention on the graph paper.

"So, what is this?" I asked.

"A sketch-up of your set pieces."

My eyebrows could not have arched any higher. "You always were such an overachiever."

"I learned from the best."

Then he pointed to each piece, explaining it in detail. His arm grazed mine, and my skin ignited.

"Looks good."

His eyes lingered on my face. "Yes, I agree."

I took a step to the side. "You sure you'll be able to finish this in time? It seems like a lot of work."

"You doubt me, Georgia? You know I enjoy a challenge as much as you do."

The temperature of the room rose by a hundred degrees. As I looked anywhere but at Weston's face, something in the corner of the room caught my eye. I walked toward it as he spoke.

"For the two weeks before school lets out for winter break, I'll have my classes working on some of these bigger pieces. And then I'll finish up the rest at my shop at home."

I nodded, only half listening.

"What are these?" I asked. On a table were tiny replicas of furniture.

"It's, uh . . . something I've been working on in my free time. For Savannah."

My hand hovered over a miniature sofa set.

"Go ahead."

I examined one of the chairs. So much detail was etched into every centimeter. He had a lot of talent . . . not surprisingly. Weston could do anything he put his mind to. He'd always been that way.

"These are beautiful."

"So is she." He cleared his throat. "I talked with her a couple of hours ago, actually. The side effects of the chemo are starting to make her pretty sick . . . but she's a trooper."

I carefully touched a dining table and chair set, thinking of the little girl who should be home playing with these, not lying in a hospital bed.

"I'm heading up to see her on Sunday. Thought maybe I could bring a couple of video clips of rehearsal to show her. It would make her happy to see what's going on."

"Sure. Whatever I can do for her."

"Thank you."

My stomach knotted at the vulnerability in his voice. I had no doubt he loved his niece, but I sensed there was something unique he shared with her.

As I turned to leave, he called my name.

"Yes?"

"If I promise to wake you up the next time you pass out on my couch, will you call me your friend?"

"You're unbelievable." I bit back a smile.

"I'll take that as a yes."

I waved before walking out of the shop.

Halfway down the hall, I heard him bellow, "O Christmas tree, O Christmas tree!"

As much as I wanted to, I couldn't suppress my giggle.

~

Five minutes into the first rehearsal, I realized why I'd never dreamed of directing.

Half a dozen students ran around the stage aimlessly, while another few texted on their phones as if life itself hung in the balance. But the worst was the group who fought over what the ideal costume should look like for each modernized character. And those were the adults! At the center of that particular argument was Sydney Parker.

It was like watching *Real Housewives of Lenox, Oregon*. I realized that every one of the women who signed up to help with costume design had been a cheerleader.

Shoot me now.

When the arguing got so out of control that I could no longer hear the voices in my head, I turned to Misty and asked whether it would be appropriate for me to wear a whistle during future rehearsals. When she laughed, I took it as a sign I was in for trouble.

Finally, I stood up. "Okay, okay! I'm going to need everyone except for my cast to step out of the theater, please. We have a lot to get done here tonight."

Sydney put her hand on her hip. "And just where are we supposed to go? We need to figure out these costumes or your cast will have nothing to wear!"

Calm down, Blondie.

"Well, why don't you try a coffee shop or maybe one of your living rooms? You have a large house, right, Syd?"

She turned the color of Pepto-Bismol and clamped her mouth shut, glancing around nervously. "Well . . . I . . . fine. Ladies, let's head to the coffee shop on eighteenth. I'll buy the drinks."

Snatching her designer purse off one of the theater chairs, she marched her crew out the side exit.

Thank God.

"All right, Mary and Joseph, please take center stage. You, there—kid with the plaid boxer briefs hanging out of his pants— please stop harassing the wise men. And . . . girl with the pink stripe in your hair, can you collect everyone's chewing gum in a waste-basket? And for the love of all that is good and holy . . . *No cell phones during rehearsal!*"

Suddenly, all eyes were on me.

Fine. Good. Perfect.

Misty gave me a thumbs-up and flashed a you-tell-'em grin my way.

"Now, please open your scripts for our first read-through. We'll do this three times tonight, and then I want this memorized by the end of the week. We have a lot of blocking and scene changes to learn. I do not want you to be fumbling with lines, understood? If you know your times tables, then you can memorize a script."

"Um . . . not everyone knows their times tables, Miss Cole," said boxer-brief boy in the back. Everyone laughed.

Gosh, I need to learn their names soon.

"Well, if you can memorize the script, I will memorize all your names. Deal?"

"Deal!"

Great. Who said teenagers are so hard, anyway? They seem perfectly lovely to me.

But by the third read-through, I was starting to have some seri-ous doubts. Four weeks. No, twenty-seven days. Maybe we should just get a giant group of kids together to sing "Frosty the Snowman" and "Jingle Bells" and call it good.

This is not LA. These are not professionals.

I tried to remind myself of that fact—many times over.

"Okay, stop." I stood and walked over to the stage, although I did not get on it.

I wasn't exactly sure what to say, but I knew I couldn't listen to another word without giving some kind of direction. It simply wasn't working. My actors sounded like . . . well . . . high schoolers.

We just stood there, staring blankly at each other, waiting for a magic solution I wasn't sure how to provide.

Um . . .

"No one sounds like they care."

I spun around.

Weston. *Naturally.*

He sauntered down the center aisle, measuring tape in hand.

"Josie, pretend like you're talking with Max whenever you have a scene with Justin. You two are supposed to be getting married. And Justin, you have to enunciate your words, bud."

He was right. *Dang it.* He was so right.

I didn't know who Max was, but given the blush on Josie's face, he was obviously someone she had a crush on.

"Okay, Mr. James," Justin said.

"Mary—I mean—Josie, let's take it from page twenty-three," I said.

They started reading again. I felt the eyes of Weston on me, but refused to turn around. Instead, I focused on the stage.

As we painfully limped to the end of the script, I heard the snap of Weston's measuring tape several times. I managed to sneak a few glances at him while he was busy scribbling on his tablet.

When we called it a wrap, the daunting amount of work left to do hit me like a punch to the gut. It was going to take a lot more than a few simple pointers. There was still music, blocking, lighting, props, costumes—

Savannah. Remember Savannah.

"Don't stress about it. It will all come together. It's Christmas-time. No one expects perfection. People just want somewhere to spend an evening with family and friends and have the opportunity to help out a great cause," Misty said.

Why doesn't that feel like enough for me?

Misty gave me a quick hug and told me she would be back tomorrow night, same time, same place.

Pulling my jacket on, I heard the lobby doors to the theater bang closed. I glanced around.

I was alone.

Weston must have left with the cast. Without saying good-bye. *Good. It's better that way.*

Shoving my hands into the pockets of my coat, I walked toward the stage, staring it down like the Goliath it had become. For being an inanimate object, it had a surprisingly intense impact on me. And just like viewing an old movie, the vivid details of my humiliation played out for me again.

Right here, on this very spot, Weston James had set me up for the last time. He'd done permanent and irrevocable damage to my heart. And I'd allowed it. I'd allowed myself to be blinded by his alluring glances, his sexy dimples, and his sultry smiles.

But it was a ruse. Just like our secret friendship had been.

Adored for his magnetic charisma, Weston had always had it easy—family, friends, girlfriends, sports, talents, you name it. He charmed the world.

But I wouldn't give in to that charm of his. Not this time.

What did I care about a missed good-bye tonight—or any other night for that matter? After all, we hadn't spoken in seven years! Hadn't I already proven to myself that I didn't need him?

I shoved my hands inside my coat pockets and turned away from the stage, fixing my gaze on a giant red-and-green wreath hanging on the back wall.

A second punch to the gut in only a few seconds.

Christmas.

Repressing the hurts that ensnared my heart around the holiday season wasn't always possible, but whatever memories I couldn't bury completely, I'd found another way to conquer.

On paper.

And thus, my career was born.

Within the limitless boundaries of my imagination, every perfect cliché of Christmas hovered on the tips of my fingers. The joy, the cheer, the happiness—all of it could be real: families gathering for traditional meals, and parents doting on their grateful children while gifting them treasures purchased with care and thought and . . . love.

Nothing could taint the Christmases I created in my mind.

No matter how my past had failed me.

And no matter *who* had failed me.

I may have lacked firsthand experience in the magic of Christmas, but my ambition to rise above my shortcomings proved stronger. Like it always had.

Nan was right: *can't* was simply not an option.

❧

I locked the theater door with the sacred key and turned to face the dark, empty parking lot.

Shoot! I forgot I walked here.

I was *so* not in LA anymore. There wasn't a single light anywhere on the street. And it was only nine.

I started walking, cursing the wind gusts that seemed to blow directly from the Arctic, and calculated how quickly a girl without gloves and a hat could last in thirty-degree weather. My hands were turning a strange shade of red, and my face had gone completely numb—*again.*

I heard a loud rumble behind me. "Hey, is your name Candy? As in Candy Cane? Want a ride?"

Despite my near hypothermia, I ignored the obnoxious but familiar voice shouting through the open window of the truck rolling up beside me.

Though I could imagine the feel of the heater vent blowing across my frostbitten skin, my willpower held out.

"Come on, stop being so stubborn. I got halfway home and realized I didn't see your car in the parking lot. You must be freezing. Get in, Georgia."

"N-n-no. I'm f-f-fine."

He laughed but continued to match my pace. "Get in, Georgia."

"W-w-e aren't-t f-friend-ds, West-ton-n."

"Fine. Whatever you say. Now, get in this truck before I throw you over my shoulder."

He stopped the truck the very millisecond I stopped walking. When I tried to grip the door handle, it snapped away from my hand, *twice*. My fingers were now beet purple, and my hands were frozen into arthritic claws. As I climbed into the seat, he turned all the heater vents toward me. I wasn't about to complain. If blood could freeze inside a living body, I was almost positive it was happening inside mine right now.

"You should remember how cold the winter nights get. You did grow up here, you know."

I didn't respond, but only because my jaw needed to defrost before I could open my mouth.

"And where are your gloves?"

I balled my hands in front of the vent and shrugged.

After a few moments, he sighed. "You'll get it, you know. Those kids on stage—you can make them great. You just need to show them you believe in them. Learn who they are. If you do that, they will give you what you want. I promise."

I shivered involuntarily. "You know *all* of them?"

"Yep. I've had every single one of them in my class at some point."

It was still so strange for me to think of Weston as a shop teacher. Weston, who had dreamed of designing buildings and skyscrapers since second grade.

He pulled into Nan's driveway and then hopped out, opening my door before I could protest.

"All you have to do is say the word, Georgia. I could help you pull this off. But I won't be ignored."

I stared at him dead-on, my earlier resolve coming back full force. "I appreciate the ride tonight and the set construction, but I'll be fine on my own."

When I started to walk toward the front door, he caught up to me and grabbed my arm, pulling me back. "When you change your mind, and you *will* change your mind, Nan has my number."

"Your cockiness is out of control."

His eyes roamed my face before fixing on my lips. "You don't really think that. You *know* me, Georgia."

I swallowed as he leaned in so close I could smell the peppermint on his breath.

His right dimple came to life as his mouth ticked up on one side. "Good night, Frost Princess. I'll see you around."

As I watched him pull away, I was no longer concerned about the chill of the air, but about the protective frozen wall around my heart . . . that was slowly beginning to melt.

CHAPTER SEVEN

The next two days and nights were Weston-free, but they were far from drama-free.

The Clash of the Cheerleaders had given me a permanent migraine, and though my actors were proving to be decent at memorizing, they spoke their lines with as much emotion as roadkill. Plus, Kevin, the boy with the ever-showing boxers, simply would not stop taunting the wise men, no matter what kind of threats I hurled his way.

I rubbed my temples and did another countdown in my head. *Twenty-five days.*

I was on edge, testy, and annoyed, but worst of all, I couldn't get a certain set of dimples out of my mind.

"Miss Cole?"

I snapped out of my mental torment.

"Yeah, Josie?"

"Is it true we have to practice every Saturday?"

I tried my best to smile sweetly. "Yes, we need to practice every day we can." *And about ninety more than that.*

"Well, I have a Christmas party I have to attend on the fourteenth. It's out of town. We go every year."

"Yeah, I have something going on that day, too," Kevin said.

"Me, too," another kid piped up.

I stood with my hands on my hips. "*All* of you have a Christmas party to attend that Saturday? You guys, that is just a week before the show. That is a *crucial* Saturday practice."

"Please, Miss Cole. We will work extra hard," Josie said.

Suddenly, I got an idea.

"Extra hard?" I asked.

The stage was filled with bobbleheads.

"Okay, a Saturday off means that you have to start taking your roles seriously. No more hawking loogies in the middle of your lines. I want to *feel* the emotion and humor and voice of each of your characters."

"So, all we have to do is become better actors, and we can have that Saturday off?"

"Yep. And Miss Peach—I mean, Mrs. Aarons—and I will be the judge of that."

Misty nodded, impressed that I finally remembered her married name.

Perfect.

❧

So, as it turns out, teenagers are the spawn of the purest kind of evil.

On Friday evening, Weston arrived at the theater, trailing behind a pack of devilish hoodlums—a.k.a. my actors.

"What are *you* doing here?" The hiss of my voice caused several glances to shoot our way.

"I'm their secret weapon, apparently."

"What are you talking about?"

"They want a Saturday off." He shrugged. "I'm gonna help them get one."

"No one cleared this with me."

"Well, Ms. Tinseltown, consider yourself informed." He hopped up on the stage with one bicep-straining motion. "All right guys, get in your places. We have a show to put on." He clapped once and shot me a not-so-innocent grin.

No way. I turned to Misty, looking for her to confirm my outrage.

"I say let him help us. He *does* know the kids, Georgia."

I closed my eyes and exhaled. Fine. *I can do this.* Weston was just one more obstacle to tackle.

A bridge to cross. A gap to jump. A mouth to kiss.

Strike that last one.

"What do you think, Miss Cole?" Weston asked.

Everyone stared at me.

I blinked. "Um . . . what was that?"

"Can the wise men add a swagger to their walks?"

The boys demonstrated this, and I nearly choked with laughter. Misty giggled uncontrollably.

"Yes . . . yes, I think that's great."

Weston winked at me and continued with his observations and ideas. Despite the sudden urge to join him up there, I remained on the floor.

"Okay, then, let's take it from the top."

As the kids took their places, Weston dropped himself into the seat next to me in the front row. And I heard Misty's snicker on my other side as he did so.

Weston leaned over and whispered in my ear, "Amazing, isn't it?"

"What is?"

"That people still know how to ask for help when they need it."

I stared straight ahead, refusing to look at the smirk on his face, although his proximity made it nearly impossible to concentrate on anything but him. Shifting in my seat, I tried to create an extra pocket of space between us.

"Shh. I'm trying to listen to my actors."

The low rumble of amusement in his chest caused my pulse to tap dance.

"If you would stop trying so hard to hate me, you might just find that you actually enjoy my company."

A little too much, probably.

છ∕૭

"You heading over to play bingo?" Weston asked as I locked the theater door.

I glanced at my phone. 8:38 p.m. I had promised Nan I would stop by the community center if I could, but Weston hadn't been part of that plan.

"Um, I'm not sure yet."

"Debating an offer for a hot date?"

I guffawed. "Definitely not."

"And what if I ask you out?"

I stopped and turned. He was grinning, obviously amused by his stupid joke. "You're so—"

"Charming, handsome, funny, witty . . . just pick your adjective."

"Irritating."

His smile widened, crinkling the corners of his eyes. "Hey . . . that's not as bad as some of the things you've called me in the past."

I opened my car door, and he walked to the passenger side. "What do you think you're doing?"

"Riding with you to bingo."

I stared at him. "Do you understand the phrase 'personal bubble'?"

"Nope."

I rolled my eyes. "I'm not staying long. Drive yourself."

"Nope." He opened the door and plopped into the seat, reclining it as he did.

Unbelievable.

"This tiny car was not made for guys my size."

He was right; he looked ridiculously cramped. His muscular build, height, and overall fatheaded arrogance were too much for my miniconvertible.

"Want to get out and take your truck?"

"You gonna ride with me?"

"Nope."

"Then drive on, Rudolph."

✌

We pulled into the community center a few minutes later, and Weston walked beside me as we entered the large hall. Fortunately, Eddy masked our entrance as she barked out the next sequence. She'd managed Bingo Fridays ever since I was a young girl. At a buck a card, the admission for the evening included unlimited soda, snacks, and popcorn. It was one of the town's biggest social events. Even popular high school students could be found here on Friday nights.

I found Nan sitting by Franklin and scooted in beside her, careful to leave no room for Weston. But true to form, he wasn't deterred. He grabbed a folding chair and set it at the table's end, turning it backward and straddling it. Our knees bumped multiple times, almost as if he were doing it on purpose.

I ignored his boyish attempts for attention, focusing instead on Nan's card.

"B-12," Eddy hollered from the stage.

"Ooh . . . you're only two away, Nan!"

She squinted at me. "You're excited about bingo? Since when?"

I'll pretend to be excited about anything to take my mind off the tingles shooting up my leg at the moment!

"Yep. I love bingo." I threw back a few pieces of popcorn, realizing for the first time that I'd missed lunch . . . and dinner. As I reached for an Oreo on Nan's plate, Weston stood up and walked off. Finally, I could breathe.

"You guys on a date?"

A giant piece of Oreo flew out of my mouth as I choked.

"What?" Nan asked, seemingly innocent. "Two days ago you couldn't stand the thought of being in the same room with him, and now, you're playing footsie with him on Bingo Friday."

"I am not!"

She laughed so hard I worried she'd rupture something important.

"What did I miss? What's so funny?" Weston set a full plate of food in front of me.

I looked up at him, completely bewildered.

"You haven't eaten, right?"

Speechless, I shook my head.

"Well, start chowing down. Mrs. Henrietta made her chicken salad sandwiches, and I know firsthand that if you don't get to them first, someone else will. They're like gold around these parts. I brought you two."

I looked down at the plate and bit my bottom lip. *Why do you do this to me, Weston?* In only a matter of minutes, I'd morphed into the kind of girl who could cry over a kind gesture like the gifting of chicken salad sandwiches.

As I stuffed my face with the random foods on the plate, Weston answered Nan's questions about Savannah's care.

"Willa said she was up most of last night vomiting, but she had a better day today. It's just really hard for her to keep anything down." I swallowed a large bite of chocolate cake and awkwardly pushed my plate away, hoping I didn't look like the most unsympathetic human being ever.

"Well, I have a few things I'd like you to take up to Portland with you on Sunday, if you don't mind. Some books. They're ones that Georgia loved when she was little."

Weston shifted his gaze to me, and a spasm rocketed through my core.

No! Stop that! Why was my body always defying me when it came to him?

"I'd love to take whatever you have for her, Nan."

"Great."

Weston's phone buzzed, and his brow furrowed.

"Hang on." He stood and walked toward the window. I couldn't help but watch him. Weston James was like a piece of fine art, one I hadn't allowed myself to fully appreciate until now. But with his eyes fixed outside and my pride momentarily banished, I surreptitiously studied the masterpiece in front of me.

"Maybe you should just take a picture—you know, with that fancy phone of yours," Eddy muttered as she sat down with us.

Flames crept up my cheeks to the tips of my ears. "I . . . I was looking out the window."

"Ha! Sure you were. That backside of his was discussed at length during my book club a few months ago."

Oy. I did not need to know that. "Okay, then."

Eddy's voice grew shriller. "What? I'm just saying—"

"We need to go," Weston said, taking my arm and pulling me up.

"What? Where?"

Was that Willa on the phone? Had something happened to Savannah?
Weston's stride was quick, my arm tucked under his. I didn't even say
good-bye to Nan. Not that I had a clue what was happening.

"I need your keys."

"Why?"

"I'll fill you in on the way. Hand them over."

I rolled my eyes and placed them in his palm.

After adjusting every single custom seat setting I had, Weston
started my car, and we were on our way. Where? I still had no clue.

"Weston, what's going on?" I buckled my seat belt.

"We're rescuing Prince Pickles."

I belted out a cough-like chuckle. "Who?"

"Savannah's dog. The neighbor called. I guess he dug out of the
backyard again. I swear, that mutt is the bane of my existence—
yippy and annoying—but Savannah loves him for some reason."
He shook his head.

"Hmm . . ."

"What?" he asked, glancing over at me.

"Nothing," I said in a sing-song voice.

Weston poked my thigh with his finger. "Tell me."

I squirmed in my seat as he repeated the gesture. "It's just
that Savannah seems to have a knack for loving exasperating
creatures . . ."

His mouth fell open in mock offense. "Oh. No. You. Didn't."

Swallowing the giggle in my throat, I pushed my door open the
second Weston parked in front of Willa's house. In no time, he was
trotting up the porch stairs after me.

"Take it back."

I shook my head. "No way."

"Georgia Cole, I'll have you know, I'm perfectly lovable—"

A shrill bark interrupted Weston's rant.

"Weston? That you?" An older man rounded the corner holding a dog that looked like the end of a dirty mop. The mutt squirmed in his arms, wagging his tail as Weston reached for him.

Apparently, Weston's feelings toward the dog weren't mutual.

"Thanks, Mr. Murphy. Sorry he got out . . . *again*."

Mr. Murphy waved him off. "No problem. I know what he means to that girl. You should tell your sister to keep better track of him."

Weston frowned at the animal now licking his cheek with unabashed pleasure. "I will, thanks again."

I laughed and shoved my frozen hands into my pockets. I waited for Weston to open the front door as Mr. Murphy walked away.

⁂

Prince Pickles went crazy the second Weston set him down. He spun in circles, his cottony hair a magnet for every piece of lint it encountered. No wonder he looked like a Q-tip dipped in soil. He ran to a room down the hall and then back out, barking at Weston's feet.

"She's not here, buddy."

The dog sobered instantly, as if that were the only explanation he needed.

I took a tentative step forward. "He understands you?"

"He has some weird doggy ESP with Savannah. I think he knew she was sick even before Willa realized it. He wouldn't leave Savannah's side for weeks . . ." Weston looked out the window as Prince Pickles laid his head on the linoleum floor.

I glanced down the hallway, fighting to squelch the uncomfortable burn at the base of my throat. I was much better at *writing* dialogue than saying it. While Weston filled Prince Pickles's water and food bowls, I studied each picture on the wall. Most were of Savannah, but a few were of Willa and Weston.

The wall of photographs was a timeline of memories, and one in particular twisted around my heart like barbed wire. I paused in front of it, taking in every detail. The background, the faces, the costumes—it was the night of the Christmas play seven years ago. There Weston stood, his arm around his sister's shoulders, beaming at the camera . . . while I was weeping alone in the playground, nursing a broken heart.

Suddenly, my skin burned with fury. *How dare he—*

"Whatcha thinking about?"

I started at the sound of his voice. My heart flung itself against the brick wall I just rebuilt.

"Can we go back now?" I asked.

"Are you okay?" Concern edged his voice.

No. In no sense of the word was I *okay*, especially not while in the presence of Weston James. "I'm fine. I just need to get going."

"*Need* to or *want* to?" He scanned my face for answers I prayed weren't there.

"Does it matter?"

"It does to me."

I rolled my eyes and hiked my satchel strap higher onto my shoulders. I squeezed past him in the tight hallway.

Peeking my head into the living room, I whispered, "Bye, Prince Pickles. I hope you get reunited with your owner soon."

The dog was safe, fed, and drooling on a large pillow.

Crisis averted. Weston didn't need me after all.

He never had.

Jerking the front door open, I made my way back to my car, unwilling to allow Weston to bully me into staying there a minute longer.

I stood outside in the cold, waiting for Weston to unlock my car with the keys he'd stolen from me, when I heard his voice.

"We're not driving anywhere until we talk."

I whipped my head around. *"What?"*

Arms folded, eyes narrowed, Weston stood with his feet planted shoulder-width on the porch steps.

"Be serious, Weston. Let's go."

"Oh, I'm serious. And if you think you're getting these keys back without wrestling me to the ground—a wrestling match I'd thoroughly enjoy, by the way—then you're crazy. It's time to talk, Georgia. Inside, where we won't die from hypothermia."

I crossed my arms over my chest, mirroring his macho demeanor. "No."

The smirk on his face churned my organs into a rage stew.

"Then what's your plan, Georgia?"

I had no plan, other than to get away from him—far, far away.

"Give me the keys." I held out my palm as a shudder racked my body from head to toe.

He arched an eyebrow. "And if I refuse?"

Before I could answer, he strode toward me and manacled his large, warm hand around my wrist. My strength faded, extracted from my being by the heart-sucking vacuum that was Weston James. My knees trembled as he raised my hand to his mouth, warming it with his breath.

And then I was transported to another lifetime.

၈

By the age of ten, Weston had more than made himself known in my life: pulling my hair, pushing me into puddles, and giggling when I misspelled a word during the spelling bee in fourth grade. But then one afternoon after school, he found me crying alone in the park.

Even though I knew he lived across the street, I wasn't worried about running into him—or anyone for that matter. No one played at the park in mid-October. It was too cold.

Leaning against the big oak tree, I shivered as tears rolled down my cheeks. My mom's most recent lecture replayed in my mind— her insensitive words, her unyielding expectations, her uncompromising demands.

When Weston slumped down beside me, I envisioned every nickname imaginable involving the word *baby* being tacked on to *Georgia* by the end of the school week. He'd mock me, tease me, ridicule me for years to come. All because the girl he saw every day at school—the one who wouldn't be caught dead showing weakness to the world, the one who had challenged him time and time again inside the safety of those four walls Monday through Friday—didn't match the girl who sat crying in the park. The girl who was so tired of compensating for her emotionally absent mother.

But Weston said nothing.

He simply lifted my hands to his mouth and warmed me from the inside out.

No words needed.

After that day, he still pestered me, of course, still sought me out in school and joked with me, but that day at the tree changed me—gave me hope.

That we could be more than just classmates.

That he could be something I'd never really had before.

A friend.

An unspoken, unexpected, friend.

⁊

Weston's inviting breath dissolved the knot that had wrapped itself around my heart and held me captive to my doubts. As his lips brushed against my fingertips, his warmth sparked my frozen core back to life. I didn't yank my hand away, or twist my arm, or elbow his wickedly attractive face. I simply thawed under his touch, berating myself for the weakness that had once again taken me over.

He reached for my other hand as if it were a piece of kindling to add to a fire—the one he'd just built inside me. "You are so stubborn."

Diverting my eyes, I exhaled shakily.

"Why do you do this, Weston?"

"Do what?"

"This?" I nodded to my hands and pulled them away from his grasp, cold seeping into my bones immediately. "Just *stop it* already. We aren't kids anymore."

His intense gaze steamrolled me. "No, we certainly are not."

Every hair on the back of my neck stood at attention. I swallowed.

"Why don't you tell me something I *don't* know, Georgia? Tell me why one day I was confessing my feelings to you and the next you pretended not to know me. Like I was suddenly some kind of creep for trying to talk to you at school . . . or anywhere."

Weston stepped closer as my backside pressed against the freezing metal of my car door.

"Maybe I got tired of being your dirty little secret, the butt of your jokes."

His jaw clenched. "What are you talking about?"

Placing my hands firmly on his chest, I pushed against him. He didn't budge an inch. Instead, he caged me in, pressing his palms to the car on either side of me.

"Don't act like you don't know what I'm talking about. I'm an expert in one-sided relationships." I practically spat the words.

Weston shook his head, and his body inched close, close, closer. "There was nothing one-sided about what we had . . . what I *thought* we had. You still owe me an explanation."

I fought against him. "*I* owe *you?* Are you kidding me? Do you even remember what happened the night of the Christmas play, when you left me lying on the floor with a ripped dress, gawking at me like you had no idea why I had just flung myself at you?" My voice cracked. "While everyone laughed . . . including you and Miss Perfect!"

Weston's eyes narrowed as he recalled the memory, a memory that was still near the forefront of *my* mind. "Why would I laugh at you? I don't even know what happened that night."

"You're unbelievable!" I took a step to the side, struggling to free myself from him. "You and Sydney tricked me. You added that last-minute scene change just to humiliate me. *Why?* So the two most popular kids in school could have one last laugh at the underdog?"

Weston flattened me against the car door, holding me captive. His breath warmed the side of my neck as I turned my head away. "I made no plans to trick you that night, Georgia—not with Sydney or anyone else. I swear to you."

I snapped my eyes back to him. "But I *saw* you wink at me—after Mr. Daniels told you about the scene change. I *saw* you! You agreed to that kiss and then let me stumble and fall off the stage!"

"No." His soft whisper caressed my cheek. "No, sweetheart. I never agreed to anything like that. Whatever you saw, it was misinterpreted."

"But Sydney said—"

"You're really going to believe her over me?"

Yes. No. Maybe?

"But why . . . *why* would Sydney do that to me?" My voice was shaky and small.

As I stared at Weston's painfully handsome face, I could think of a few reasons.

Sydney had always wanted Weston—to be crowned senior-prom queen and king with him, to be Lenox's little couple of popularity and perfection.

But Weston hadn't wanted that. He'd been too busy rehearsing for the lead in the winter play to think about that, too busy spending his extra time with me.

"I wish I knew, Georgia."

A sob caught in my throat. "But you *did* know how I felt about you . . ."

The weight of his body against mine made my stomach spasm. "Remind me. How did you feel?"

Shaking my head, I closed my eyes for a long second under the scrutiny of his gaze. His lips were a mere millimeter from mine. "It doesn't matter now. My feelings weren't real."

The tip of his nose traced my jaw. As he worked his way past my earlobe, I struggled to breathe.

"Oh, I think they were very real . . . *are* very real."

I shuddered as his hands cradled my face.

"You were never my dirty little secret, Georgia." He studied me, unblinking. "I knew then what I know now. You're special, unique, and as beautiful on the inside as you've always been on the outside. Maybe I never wanted to share you with anyone . . . maybe I still don't."

As Weston's lips feathered against my forehead, all the anger, frustration, and bitter resentment departed from me with a single exhalation.

"You've always been more than just a *friend* to me, Georgia Cole. I only wish it hadn't taken seven years of silence for you to believe that."

Weston pulled me into his chest, wrapping his strong arms around me as my fantasy fused with reality.

I snuggled deep into his thermal shirt like it was the shelter I'd spent a lifetime trying to find. "I do, too . . . I'm sorry."

He stroked my hair softly. "I was a stupid boy to let you walk out of my life so easily, Georgia, but I won't be a stupid man." He kissed the top of my head. "I won't be a stupid man."

Chapter Eight

I groggily reached for my phone on the nightstand, ready to press snooze, when I realized it was a phone call, not my alarm. I looked at the clock—it was 5:46 a.m.

My mom.

"Hi, Summer."

She'd asked me to start calling her by her first name after she had the twins.

"Hey, were you sleeping?"

I yawned. "Well, you *are* three hours ahead of me."

She laughed, dismissing her absentmindedness without a second thought. "Nan told me you're staying there for Christmas?"

"Yes, I am."

"You should have made up an excuse. I bet you're ready to be back in LA getting on with your life."

I felt a prick of defensiveness at her words. She hated it here . . . or maybe just the memories that *here* held for her. I'd probably never know for sure.

"It hasn't been that bad."

She huffed. "Well, you never told me what happened with your last script. The one with the schoolteacher set in the 1940s."

It was a screenplay I'd written a couple of years ago, one my agent had requested. Although it was still in the holiday genre, it showcased a bit more of my talent than some of the others.

"I haven't heard anything about it yet. It takes awhile sometimes."

"Well, I'm sure it will at least be picked up for another Hallmark movie. Just remember, this is when you pay your dues. You've got to stick with it. You have a good thing going. It usually takes a long time for people to find a niche like you've created for yourself."

I knew I shouldn't have told her I'd been thinking about pursuing something different.

"I'm grateful for what's happened so far, really." *Even if I'm bored to tears with it.*

"Good. Just don't go changing things up now. Stay the course, and work hard. It will pay off."

What she really meant was, "Don't try and write other genres. Don't get too creative or impulsive. Don't mess this up."

"How are the kids?" I asked, changing the subject.

"Great. Brad and I are going to take them to Disney World for New Year's. Just bought the hotel package."

"Aren't they a little young for that?"

"What? No. It will be a good family memory for all of us."

Family. Hearing her say the word stung, like pouring Tabasco sauce on an open wound.

"Good. I'm glad you're happy."

She paused for a few seconds. I could hear a small voice calling her in the background. "You'll find one someday, too, Georgia."

"Find what?"

"A family of your own."

You were supposed to be my family, Mom.

છ

I stood in the shower for a long time—so long that Nan finally rapped on the door to check on me. When the scorching-hot water turned lukewarm and eventually cold, I got out, wrapped myself in a fuzzy towel, and padded down the hallway.

"Um . . . I'll just . . ."

I whirled around to see the source of the voice behind me. "Oh my gosh! Weston!"

Running to my room, I slammed the door, which banged open and closed four times before actually latching shut. I rested my head against the door, and my heart raced as I tried to recall exactly how my towel had been positioned when I left the bathroom.

"I didn't see anything! Promise!" he yelled down the hall. "Nan said she told you I was here before she left. Sorry!"

Was that what she had said?

I bit my lip, shaking my head. And then . . . I laughed. Hard. For whatever reason, God had decided that Weston James was my personal humility meter.

By the time I dressed in skinny jeans, a sweater, and boots, my earlier dour mood had lightened considerably. Though Weston and I were still firmly in the "It's complicated" phase, last night had radically changed something in me. I wasn't sure what it meant yet, but I was willing to find out.

"Hey, you." He smiled and held my jacket out to me.

"Hey." I was still blushing from the hallway scene.

"Thought we might grab a quick cup of coffee before rehearsal. Is that okay?"

My smile seemed to pull from all directions. "Yeah, that sounds good."

We took his truck to Brew It & Company and found a table by the window after we ordered.

"I have something for you," he said, reaching into his leather jacket.

"You do?"

"Although I think I might be shooting myself in the foot by giving it to you. I kind of like *my* remedy for keeping you warm."

I eyed him curiously as he placed a small paper bag from Gigi's Grocery on the table. I picked it up, intrigued.

Gloves.

Weston James bought me a pair of gloves?

I looked up at him, words escaping me. Something in the back of my throat burned.

"Hey, you okay? I only got black because I didn't know what other color you'd want."

"Thank you." My words were thin, shaky. "Really, thank you for these."

He touched my arm. "I know we can't go back in time, Georgia, but I don't want to waste any time now."

I nodded. "Me, either."

His eyes crinkled. "You know . . . you're pretty adorable when you're not hating my guts."

Leaning in closely, I whispered, "Don't get used to it."

He laughed.

And so did I.

⁂

Misty couldn't make it to practice that day because her youngest was home sick with the stomach flu. In that moment, I was extremely grateful for Weston's help.

It was the first day of blocking. As usual, I directed from the floor while Weston assisted the cast onstage.

"No, a little more to the left. And the shepherds need to be a lot farther back on stage right. Yep . . . right there is good."

Weston taped and marked as the kids rehearsed their places over and over.

"What about the angel? You gonna try to lower him down?" Weston asked.

I tilted my head and squinted, imagining how it all might play out. This was the most important scene because it was Savannah's favorite.

"I'd like to. Do you think we can rig it?"

Weston beamed with confidence. "Absolutely."

The hours ticked by. Everyone ate sack lunches during a fifteen-minute break, and then we were back at it. No rest for the weary—or the holidayed out. That was my own personal motto, anyway.

"It's four," Weston called out.

Seriously? How did the time go by so fast?

"Um . . . okay. Let's meet back here Monday after school, and then we will lengthen practices when winter break starts next week."

Several kids exclaimed in glee while others groaned. I could empathize with both responses.

As the last student exited, Weston made a move toward me, and my heart skipped an extra beat or two . . . or maybe ten.

"We have a problem." He read the question in my eyes. "I can't continue practicing in this theater every day knowing the truth behind your stage fright." He shook his head. "Especially when you've believed all these years that I arranged that prank. That seriously kills me, Georgia."

I swallowed hard. "Well, it wasn't exactly pleasant for me, either."

He stopped a few inches in front of me. "I think we need to make it right."

I laughed. "What? How can we possibly do that? It was seven years ago, Weston."

He held out his hand. "Let me take you up on stage."

"I don't want to go up there."

Angling his head to the side, he flashed a grin, and a lazy dimple winked at me. "You've never been afraid of anything, Georgia. Don't start now. Come on, we'll do it together."

Grabbing my hand, he pulled me toward the stairs.

"No, seriously. I don't want to go up there." I tugged my hand away.

"Georgia, what happened that night was not your fault."

No, but I finally know whose fault it was. A certain blond witch-of-a-woman who apparently has never been told no. By anyone.

"It wasn't yours, either." The words felt strange coming out of my mouth, so opposite of my feelings for so many years.

"So, let's have a do-over. We both deserve one."

I rolled the idea around in my mind. "Fine."

"That's my girl."

I pursed my lips to avoid the smile that threatened to break through. And then we were standing on the stage, looking out at the empty seats below us.

"See? It's not so awful."

My knees started to shake—quite literally. "Okay, I'm done now."

He laughed and pulled me back. "No, you're not. Let's do the scene."

"What? You've got to be joking. I don't even know—"

"Bull. You know it. You've probably replayed it in that brain of yours a thousand times. Now, go over there, and walk toward me."

I gawked at him, waiting for him to say, "Just kidding."

Only he wasn't kidding.

In a matter of seconds, I was walking toward him, saying the lines that had been lost in a sea of laughter seven years ago. It took me only a second to get into character. He was right. I knew these lines, almost as well as I remembered the character I played.

"I don't want your warning, Patrick. I don't need it."

"You need it more than you realize, Catherine. If you marry him, he will ruin you and your family forever."

"Is that all you have to say to me?" I took another timid step toward Weston as he beckoned me closer with his hand. I knew what he wanted me to do, but I wasn't sure I could do it.

"What more do you want me to say? That I'll have you? That I'll be yours forever? I've said that with every look and every word I've ever spoken to you. You just haven't been listening."

And then . . . I let go.

I ran toward him, only this time—*this time*—Weston caught my waist and swung me around as I laughed, my head tipped back in unadulterated bliss.

Freedom.

As he slowly lowered me to the ground, his eyes drank me in. My knees weakened once more, but this time for a very different reason. Our silent stare sought the answer to one question, one that seemed to exist under my skin, through the fibers of my muscles, and in the marrow of my bones.

Could Weston James and Georgia Cole be more than secret friends?

And then his lips were on mine, his hands climbing from my hips to my face in tender expectation. As his thumbs caressed my cheekbones, Weston held me close, allowing his kiss to wash away my every doubt.

Yes. The answer was clear. *Yes, they could.*

CHAPTER NINE

I used to buy a new pair of slippers every few months. Not because I needed them, but because the moment I placed my feet inside the warm and fuzzy slippers, I imagined I was walking on clouds.

That's how I felt Sunday morning. Like I was cloud walking.

"I don't think that smile has left your face all morning."

I bit my lower lip under Nan's scrutiny and slipped on the gloves Weston bought for me.

"You riding with me to church this morning?" Nan asked.

"Yeah, and then I think I'm going to visit Savannah with Weston."

Nan clapped her hands in delight. "I just knew you two could resolve whatever silly quarrel got between you."

I looked at her. "It wasn't silly, Nan. But my anger was misdirected."

"Well, whatever it was, I hope you will let it go for good and see each other with new eyes."

"I hope so, too, Nan. I really do."

She pulled me in for a quick hug, and we were off to church.

℘

Weston bumped my hip with his while I talked to several old acquaintances in the church lobby. Apparently, he was ready to get on the road. I couldn't blame him. He hadn't seen his niece in over a week, and from what I'd gathered, that was a very long time for him.

"Finally! I thought I'd never get you to shut up back there."

I smacked his chest and climbed inside his truck. "You're such a gentleman, really."

As we pulled out of the church parking lot and drove down Main Street, we passed Sydney in her white SUV. I waved at her through the window, and she gaped when she saw me in Weston's truck. I couldn't help but feel a tad victorious.

"So, tell me about your life in LA. We have two hours to catch up on the last seven years, and I want to make them count."

"You do, huh?"

"I do."

He picked up my hand and brought it to his mouth. My heart leaped out of my chest as he kissed the back of it. "I keep picturing a certain moment last night, and I want to find out who my competition is back in Plastic Land."

"Plastic Land?"

"Hollywood."

I laughed so hard I nearly choked. "Well, I keep pretty busy with writing, and no, I don't have a boyfriend, if that's what you're asking."

He flashed that boyish grin I'd known since toddlerhood. "It's what I'm asking."

I shook my head at his antics. "And what about you, O great bachelor of Lenox?"

His smile flatlined. "You're still the only girl I've ever cared about, Georgia."

And just like that, I was fifteen again, writing secret scribbles in my diary.

Georgia Cole + Weston James = True Love.

"There's no way you haven't dated," I said, trying to forget the strength of my adolescent hormones.

"Sure. But let's just say I'm a two-date kinda guy. You have to be pretty special to get a third."

"And how many of those have there been?"

"I'm hoping you'll be the first. Today can mark numero uno."

Swirling hearts, rainbows, and flowers filled my head quicker than I could stop them. He never was the beat-around-the-bush type. Probably his best quality—if you didn't count his eyes, lips, or backside.

"So, you like it there?"

"Where? Hollywood?" I sighed. *How honest should I be?* "I'm grateful for what's happened in my career. It was a good move for me."

"Could you write from somewhere else?"

My stomach tightened at his question. Sure, it was possible, but this all felt so surreal. Too quick, too intense, too—

"Georgia, come on. Don't freak out on me. I'm just curious. It's not like I'm proposing."

"Don't joke like that."

"Why not?" He grabbed my hand that was resting on the middle console in an effort to relax my tense posture. "Just because we started over with a clean slate doesn't mean I have to throw out a lifetime of knowing you. You'll be hard-pressed to get rid of me now."

"I don't want to get rid of you. I just . . . I don't want to rush anything, okay?"

He sat quietly for a moment and then threaded his fingers through mine. "We can take it as slow as you need to, but just so you know, I'm *in this*, Georgia."

I am, too . . . and that's what scares me.

✑

During our two-hour trip to Doernbecher Children's Hospital in Portland, Weston filled me in on his move to Lenox after Willa's husband passed away. He'd only planned on taking a semester off, but he decided to stay when Willa's depression worsened during her pregnancy. I knew they'd been close, but I hadn't realized just *how* close. When he described his relationship with Savannah, I had to blink away tears. He truly loved her as if she were his own daughter.

When we arrived at the hospital, Weston carried the gift bags and box of books from Nan through the halls of the cancer ward. I glanced around at all the whimsical sculptures and birds hanging from the ceiling. Truly, the hospital looked like a fairy-tale world.

Nervous energy ran through my veins as we rode the elevator up to Savannah's room. I couldn't shake the feeling that I was invading a very personal moment, one that should be shared only with close family.

When we reached her room, I turned to tell Weston I would wait in the hallway for him, but he announced me before I had the chance.

"I brought you a special treat, Vannie."

Weston pulled me inside the sunshine-yellow room, prints of daisies and flower gardens on the walls. Willa sat in a rocking chair in the corner, and Mrs. James, Weston's mom, was washing something in the sink.

"Hey, Mom." Weston kissed her on the cheek and set Savannah's loot down on a counter. I stood awkwardly, smiling at the tired-looking little girl.

"Hi, Georgia," Willa and Mrs. James said in unison.

"Hi, um, I hope it's okay that I'm here. I don't want to intrude."

"We're *happy* to have you here," Willa said. She embraced me quickly and turned toward her daughter. "Uncle Wes brought you a friend, Vannie."

The little girl smiled. "You got my drawing?"

My throat tightened as my heart swelled. "I did. In fact, I designed the whole show around that pretty picture. Your artwork inspired me."

Savannah beamed, her sweet dimples coming to life and resembling those of the man who stood at her side. He leaned over and kissed her forehead, speaking softly into her ear. Her eyes sparkled, although there were dark circles beneath them.

Weston pulled up a stool and took her hand in his. The sight overwhelmed me. *Who was this kindhearted man? Had he always been this way? Had I missed it somehow between our fights and flirtations?*

"Wes," Willa said, "Mom and I haven't had lunch yet. Would you mind staying here while we go down to the cafe?"

"Sure thing."

"Did you want to come along, Georgia? You're welcome to."

I looked to Weston, unsure of the correct response. *Where would I be less of a burden today?*

"I want her to stay," said a soft, sweet voice.

Everyone looked at Savannah.

It was in that moment that I understood why Nan had opted to stay home from Hawaii, why an entire town would be willing to raise funds for her care during a busy holiday season, and why Weston would put aside his dreams so he could watch her grow up.

My voice diminished by half. "I'd love to stay."

I pulled up a chair to the side of her bed opposite Weston and watched as he gave her the books Nan sent with us. I saw one—*Madeline*—that I'd loved as a young girl: I was inspired by her adventures, her friends who eventually became her family, and her imagination.

"Ooh, these are from Nan?" she asked.

I nodded. "Yep, and actually, they were mine when I was young."

Her eyes smiled. "Will you read me one?"

"I sure will."

I read Savannah two books while Weston held her cold hand in his and laughed at all the funny scenes.

"I like your silly voices," she said. "That's how my teacher, Mrs. Maple, reads, too."

Weston leaned over and kissed her temple. "You should probably rest, sweetie. We'll stay here with you, though, okay?"

She started to close her eyes, her voice trailing off as she spoke. "I always wanted to meet you. Cuz of our names . . ."

And then she was asleep.

I looked to Weston for clarification, but his eyes were glued to Savannah's resting face. I sat quietly, waiting for whatever Weston wanted to do next. It didn't feel like my place to ask questions or make small talk.

Now that she was asleep, I glanced around the room, taking it all in: the IVs in her arm, the uneaten food on her plate, the container beside her bed that was obviously meant for unexpected bouts of nausea.

"I hate this." Weston dropped his head into his hands and pulled at his hair.

"I know," I whispered.

"Why *her*? I mean, I believe God has a purpose and a plan for everything, but this—what's the good that comes from a child having cancer?"

I couldn't even begin to understand the reason. I couldn't fathom why God would allow something like this to happen to someone so precious. I'd always been one to have a lot of questions but not many answers.

I reached over Savannah's still form and held my hand out for Weston. He took it.

"Thanks for coming with me today." His eyes pierced mine with a mixture of vulnerability and strength.

"Is she asleep?" Willa's voice broke the spell. I pulled my hand away, tucking it back into my lap.

"Yes, she just dozed off a minute ago. Georgia read her a couple of books."

"Oh, I bet she loved that," Mrs. James said, smiling at me kindly.

I watched them interact for the next hour or so while Savannah slept, and one thought looped over and over again in my mind: *this is a family.*

I'd always had a special relationship with Nan—she was the most important person in my life to date—but still, I'd always ached for something more.

"You ready?" Weston asked me after saying good-bye to Savannah, his sister, and his mother.

I nodded, my voice lost somewhere inside my longing for a fantasy family I'd never have.

℘

The ride home to Lenox was far less playful than the ride to Portland had been. We were both preoccupied with our thoughts of

91

Savannah. And though we stopped for gas and grabbed a quick bite to eat, we had little to say. I wanted to be sensitive to Weston. He had a lot to process, and who was I to interfere with that?

Halfway home, he picked up my hand and broke the silence. "Your mom had twins a few years ago, right?"

Startled, I pulled myself from my introspective stupor. "Yes."

"And you never considered moving there—to Florida, I mean?"

Was that a note of accusation I heard in his voice? "No."

"How come?"

"We aren't like that."

"Like what?"

Sighing an I-wish-you-would-drop-this sigh, I said, "Like . . . normal."

His chuckle rumbled low. "What is *normal* when it comes to family?"

"I don't really want to talk about this, okay?"

"Hmm." He was doing it again, that scrutinizing thing he does when he thinks he knows me better than I know myself.

"What's that supposed to mean?"

"Nothing." He shrugged diplomatically. "I'm just analyzing you is all."

"Well, you can stop. I don't need a shrink."

"Maybe not a shrink. But maybe someone to talk to?"

I shook my head and pulled my hand from his. "Let's talk about your shop class."

Weston slowed his truck as we turned off the highway toward Lenox. "Let's talk about why you make a living writing about clichés that are nothing like your life."

"How do you even know *what* I write?" I shot back, my heart pounding.

"I've read every script you've published, Georgia . . . not to mention the cheesy Christmas specials I've watched on TV."

The intimacy meter in the truck skyrocketed to the "Approach with Caution" level.

"And that makes you an expert on me?"

His gaze roamed my face. "Well, am I right? Are you obsessed with clichés because you feel some sort of pent-up resentment about your own life and childhood?"

I swallowed, my palms starting to sweat. *No. Yes. Maybe.*

"I remember the relationship you had with your mom growing up was sort of . . . strange. She seemed pretty controlling."

"She just wanted the best for me. You don't know her." *Am I seriously defending her?*

"No, I don't. But I do know you."

"You keep saying that, Weston. But seven years can change a person a great deal. We grew up. We had experiences apart from each other. We're not who we were in high school anymore."

He was quiet as we pulled into Nan's driveway.

He put the truck in park. "I don't want to fight with you, I'm sorry. I just want to understand you . . . to know what I've missed." He leaned over the seat and touched my chin, tilting my face to his. "You're right. I knew Georgia the girl . . . but the stunning woman sitting next to me now is no longer a girl."

I let out a tension-filled breath and inhaled Weston's fresh scent of wood chips, ocean, and leather—a scent so distinguishable it could make even a dead heart beat again. He brushed his lips across mine and kissed me gently.

"I want you to know her, too," I whispered.

He kissed me again.

I didn't need a new pair of slippers to go cloud walking anymore. I only needed Weston James . . . and his kisses.

Chapter Ten

By the second week in December, everything was on schedule . . . except for the snowfall. Though the temperature had dropped below freezing, precipitation remained elusive. There had been slush on the streets when I first arrived in Lenox, but no new snow had fallen.

The enormous mountain range to the east glistened with white, having experienced a fresh dousing of winter's finest blessing over the weekend. And I secretly hoped it would come our way soon. I might love the year-round sunshine of California, but standing in a fluttering of snowflakes was one childish indulgence I'd never give up.

I drove down Main, noting the lights woven through every tree and bush that lined the street. Wreaths and garlands, sleighs and reindeer, Nativities and baby Jesuses filled the town. Lenox was one giant holiday show.

After turning onto Maple, I pulled into Weston's driveway. He'd asked for my final approval on some of the smaller set pieces and props at his workshop. The larger pieces were still at school for his class to finish prior to winter break. It sounded like they were making great progress.

But my stomach plummeted when I saw a familiar SUV parked across the street. Tugging my coat tighter, I stepped out of my car. I was three steps outside his shop when I heard an unmistakable blend of voices. I pressed my ear to the door and strained to hear.

Why is Sydney Parker here?

Just then, the high-pitched scream of a saw blade pierced my eardrum, and the door jerked open. I stumbled forward, steadying myself on the massive Louis Vuitton bag slung over Sydney's shoulder. Once I righted myself, I forced a tolerant smile—though the disdain I felt for her at that moment was hardly smile worthy.

"Georgia?" Her eyes widened briefly before shrinking to two tiny slits.

What was she talking to Weston about?

Although we'd never been friends, I'd never considered her an enemy—until now.

Her jealous little prank had cost me seven years without Weston. *Seven years!* That was hardly a forgivable sin. *Right, God?*

I didn't wait around for an answer.

Pulling the door closed behind her, she guarded the entrance to the shop with her surgically enhanced and artificially tanned body. She flashed me a phony grin, nearly blinding me with the shade of her Chiclet-white teeth. *What I wouldn't give for a black light right now.*

"Why are *you* here?" Her words were clipped, dipped in candy-coated poison.

I wanted nothing more than to ask the same of her.

"Weston asked me to come over," I said, hoping to shock the snotty expression off her face. Didn't happen.

"Old flames rarely rekindle, Georgia."

"It seems I could say the same to you, Syd."

She sucked in a sharp breath. "I don't know what you're implying—"

NICOLE DEESE

"Oh, yes, you do." Three blinks and two shallow breaths later, I knew exactly what I wanted to say to Sydney Parker. "You may have driven me out of this town once by blaming Weston for your jealous deceptions, but I can assure you, it won't happen twice. Whatever game of intimidation you're bent on playing to make this town bow to your every whim, you can count me out. I don't care who your ex-husband is, or where you live, or how much money is in your bank account. This isn't high school anymore, Sydney. Mean girls don't win."

For a moment, all she could do was blink and swallow and blink again.

"Be careful, Georgia. This may not be Hollywood, but Lenox is going somewhere, and I'm the one blazing the trail. You don't want me as an enemy. Trust me."

Then, with a single huff, she marched down the driveway. Taking in a deep breath, I tried to dispel the toxic aura she had left behind.

I stepped inside Weston's shop, and the shrill sound of the saw blade ceased. I watched as Weston hunched over his desk, studying a set of blueprints and pushing his hand through his shaggy dark locks. An uneaten sandwich lay beside him. Lord only knows how old *that* was.

"Should I come back later?"

He jumped. It only took him a half second to steady himself, and once he did, his gaze roamed over me lazily, from my feet to my face.

"You look nice."

A bubble of laughter escaped me. "I'm in yoga pants."

"Yes, well, not quite as nice as you looked in the towel but still." He shrugged, his eyes teasing.

I picked up a pencil from a shelf and threw it at his chest. He caught it easily before it could make contact. *Dang those reflexes.*

"So . . . I just talked to Sydney in the driveway. Are you two friends?" I hoped my tone was casual, but as soon as I spoke her name, a bitter taste filled my mouth.

"I wouldn't call us friends. She was just dropping off some plans for me to look over." His eyes searched mine. "There's no reason to feel jealous, Georgia. *I promise.*"

A rush of sweet relief washed over me. "I'm not jealous."

He laughed. "Good."

As he brushed sawdust off his blueprints, I glanced around his workshop—a converted garage with tables, saws, workbenches, and more tools than I could name. It was quite impressive.

"I'm glad you came. I'll have my students start painting these tomorrow if you sign off on them."

"Wow, I feel so important."

His arms encircled my waist as he leaned his chin on my shoulder. "You *are* important."

His touch had always made me feel invincible—at ten, at seventeen, and even now at twenty-five. Age wasn't a factor. The security and comfort I found in Weston's touch would never change.

"Yes, well, the jury's still out on that."

He spun me around and kissed me while I giggled.

"Stop laughing," he scolded, as he continued to plant soft kisses all over my face. "I'm doing something very wrong if you find my skills so hilarious."

I just laughed harder. Then something caught my eye, and I gave Weston's chest a hefty push.

"Oh my gosh."

I knelt in front of the most beautiful dollhouse I'd ever seen. It was amazing. No, it was incredible. I blinked away the tears filling my eyes.

"The tiny furniture at the school . . . it goes with this?" I asked, touching the porch steps. Weston appeared behind me, carefully spinning the house around so I could see inside. The details were so intricate. The staircase, the windows, the bedrooms . . . all of it—breathtaking.

"It's for Savannah. For Christmas."

I ran my fingers along the textured roofline. "You're so talented."

As his eyes locked with mine, heat flooded my face. Holding his hand out to me, he pulled me into a standing position. My chest contracted, like I was suddenly breathing through an accordion. I could feel my pulse thrum hard in my neck and wondered if he could see the way his presence affected me. Toe to toe we stood, staring at each other as if the last seven years had passed in a single blink. His finger traced my jawline, dipped to my chin, and came to rest under the curve of my bottom lip. "You're no amateur yourself, Queen of the Red and Green."

He leaned in, his lips grazing my cheek as his breath tickled the sensitive skin beneath my ear. "I always knew you'd blow this town away." He exhaled into my hair, and my legs trembled.

A thousand words flittered through my mind, yet I couldn't catch even one.

Weston pulled back slightly and scanned my face in a way that both touched my soul and seared my heart.

"I'm so proud of you—of all you've accomplished," he said.

My throat burned with unshed tears. "Thank you, Weston. That means . . . so much."

He kissed my forehead and then gently tilted my chin to his. Our lips connected for several seconds of head-dizzying perfection. He pulled back. "I should probably show you the sets, huh?"

"Probably," I said, hoping he couldn't detect the disappointment in my voice.

I could have stayed in his arms the rest of the evening.

❧

"I just don't think it fits," Misty whispered to me.

"I know." I scratched my head. "I'll take care of it."

She nodded, but she expressed her lack of confidence in my people skills in the way she scrunched her nose at me.

Though I handed Betty full rein of all musical aspects of the production, I now regretted that decision the way one regrets wearing suede in a rainstorm. I had expected Christmas classics to be sung intermittently throughout the production: "The First Noel," "Angels We Have Heard on High," "Silent Night."

I had *not* expected 'N Sync's 1998 Christmas album. Apparently, we had different interpretations of the term *modern*.

I approached her with caution. "Um, Betty?"

She pounded away on the piano, not hearing me.

"Betty?" I tried again.

More pounding.

I tapped her on the shoulder. She jumped, her sheet music falling to the ground.

"Oh, I'm sorry." I knelt down and gathered up the pages, cringing at the titles.

"Were you trying to get my attention?" Betty asked sweetly.

"Yes, actually. Can we talk for a moment, please?"

"Right now? We're just about to start 'Kiss Me at Midnight.'"

"Yeah . . . I think we should probably talk before that."

❧

It didn't go well.

"Was that Betty who just left? She almost plowed me over in the parking lot." Weston sat down next to me.

I put my head in my hands as Misty stood up. "Want me to tell the kids to run it again from the top, Georgia?"

I nodded.

Weston's face was open with curiosity. "So, what happened?"

"I suck as a human being is what happened."

He laughed. "Okay?"

"Betty quit."

"*What?* Why? Isn't she doing *all* the music?"

I raised my head and stared at him. "*Was*—as in *past tense.* Again, I suck as a human being."

"I'm sure we can fix it."

I shook my head. "Somehow she translated *Modern Mary* to mean nineties pop music and not the traditional Christmas carols I had envisioned."

His mouth opened and closed twice before he finally said, "Um . . . wow, how did that happen?"

"Again, I suck—"

"As a human being. Got it. So, you didn't communicate your expectations to her?"

I shook my head, ashamed at such a rookie mistake. "We have no music now. None."

He put his arm around my shoulders. "Don't fret, my cute little elf. We'll figure this out."

"Do you have a list of annoying Christmas nicknames to call me?"

"Who needs a list when one is gifted with such an astounding brain?"

I sighed, the reality of our predicament taking its toll. "I don't know what to do."

"Well, I have someone in mind, but you should probably make peace with Betty before we ask that person to fill her place, this being a small town and all."

True. "Who?"

He winked. "Someone you know quite well, actually."

My hope surged.

Of course. Nan.

❧

It was Ladies' Book Club night at Nan's house. I'd offered to help with dinner since she'd been working so hard organizing bake sales and fund-raisers, not to mention keeping up with her piano lessons at the chapel. And it was the least I could do since I'd just added Christmas Pageant Accompanist to her list of titles.

"I can't believe you *wanted* to stay," I whispered to Weston in the kitchen.

"And miss such a great opportunity to build up my ego?"

"You hit the ceiling on that one in the fifth grade, pal. Your ego is at max capacity."

He popped a walnut in his mouth and grinned. "So . . . I was wondering."

"Yeah?" I grabbed the dressing from the fridge.

"When can I take you out for date number two?"

"I don't know. I have a pretty full schedule with the play and the old ladies' dinners and—"

Weston leaned on the counter to reduce the space between us. "Let me rephrase that. Can I take you out after your service here is complete?"

"I think that could be arranged." I bit my cheeks to conceal my delight.

"Good, because I was going to persuade a room full of old ladies to turn on you if you'd said no."

From the living room, Eddy hollered, "Georgia . . . you're not going to toss that salad dressing with the salad, right? I'm watching my levels again."

"Uh, I can leave it out."

Weston's wide smile was out of control. He looked like a child trying to hide a secret.

"And grab that low-sodium stuff in the door of the fridge, all right? But check the date first. I don't want any expired stuff. The way Nan keeps her stockpiles of condiments I can never be too sure."

"Eddy, your eyes can't read those tiny dates any better than mine can," Nan retorted.

Weston put his fist to his mouth to mute his snickering.

"Behave." I turned away from him to keep my giggles at bay.

"Oh, and Margaret can't have dairy," Eddy called out again.

I looked down at the lasagna that Weston had just pulled from the oven and shrugged in bewilderment. I entered the dining room several minutes later, and ten women watched me as I approached the table with the salad. Weston carried the main dish.

"I'm sorry, Margaret. I wasn't aware of your dairy sensitivity. I'm afraid tonight's entrée is lasagna."

"It's okay, I'll just try to eat around the cheese," Margaret said unconvincingly.

Pearl lifted the top layer of her lasagna, as if inspecting it for termites. "But it doesn't have spinach in it, right? I can't do spinach anymore . . . It makes me bloat."

Margaret piped up again, "That's what cheese does to me. Only I usually end up in the bathroom for quite a long time after."

"Ladies, ladies," Nan said, hands in the air. "Let's not scare my granddaughter. She has a nice long cheese-and-spinach-filled life ahead of her. Thank you, darlin', for this meal. It looks wonderful."

The ladies nodded their heads and murmured their thanks. Nan winked at me.

"Now, run along, dear. Go have fun—and eat whatever your healthy heart desires."

"Ooh . . . is she dating that teacher with the nice backside?" Pearl asked.

Weston winked at me as I tried to hide my blushing cheeks. His eyes danced with amusement. "Shall we?"

"*Please.* Let's get out of here."

ℰↄ

At Jonny's Pizza, Weston smirked at me across the table.

"What?" I said, with a mouth full of pepperoni goodness.

"I offer to take you anywhere you want within a sixty-mile radius, and you pick Jonny's Pizza."

"I haven't had it in seven years." I took a drink of my Diet Dr Pepper.

"What else have you missed?"

I glanced out the window. "The mountains."

"Yeah? They are pretty spectacular. We should go up there sometime."

"Really? I'd love that. But I have to tell you, I don't have the coordination for skiing or snowboarding. I'm purely a tubing kind of gal."

Weston leaned back in his chair. "We may have to remedy that someday."

The word sent my heart into a flurry. *Someday.* As in longer than my holiday stay in Lenox?

"You know I leave on the second of January, right?" The urge to clarify was too strong to deny. Regardless of what was going to happen between us, I needed to lay all my cards on the table.

"Yes, I know." Weston's eyes were void of expression.

I scooted my plate away and slid my soda glass toward me. "I mean . . . I'm having a great time with you, Wes. I'm glad I came back to visit, but I *live* in LA. My career is there."

As he raked his hand through his dark waves, I wished I could break into his thoughts and pull them out one by one. But then his stare captured mine.

"How about we just agree to see what happens, okay? I know that brain of yours wants to figure everything out and make a plan, but I just want to enjoy this—*enjoy you.*" He held my hand and rubbed the back of it with his thumb. "I like you, Georgia Cole. A whole lot."

Heat crept up my neck at the touch of his hand on mine. "I think I can do that."

"Good, because I really want to take you on a third date."

CHAPTER ELEVEN

Bags in hand, I left Gigi's Grocery and fought my way through the arctic wind gusts to my car. It was freezing out. Mid-December was upon us, and the storm of the season was supposed to hit within the next day or so. I told Nan I would stock up on all the essentials just in case. So far, though, there hadn't been a single snowflake. The weather forecasters in Oregon were overpaid.

"Miss Cole? Is that you?"

A pretty woman with long dark hair jogged over to me, pulling her coat tightly across her chest.

"Yes . . . hi, do we know each other?"

The woman had rosy lips and round cheeks. "No, but you know my daughter, Josie McDonald."

"Ah, yes. I can see the resemblance. She's a great girl. Glad she's our Mary," I said, shivering.

"I just want to thank you for what you've done for those kids—my daughter especially. It's easy to find trouble, even in a small town like ours. I've never known her to be passionate about anything in the arts until you got here. You've inspired her, really. She was so excited about getting into drama when she got to the high school, but then the program was cut. She talks about you every night when she comes home."

My limbs tingled with warmth as I pictured Josie. She had said only a few sentences to me outside of our rehearsal time, but I'd noticed she'd had a new dedication to her role over the last week. She'd even volunteered to help lead some of the younger kids in a chorus of "Silent Night" at the end of the pageant. Nan had told me a little about Josie's family after practice one night—a dad who abandoned them, a brother who was into drugs.

Suddenly, I realized what this play meant to the kids in it. It wasn't just about raising the funds to pay for Savannah's cancer treatments anymore; the arts reached a much broader audience, offering hope and healing to the community at large.

Growing up, I had used writing, reading, and drama as outlets, too; they were really the only viable outlets I *had*.

"It's my pleasure. Thank you for sharing that with me."

"You're welcome. I wish someone would buy that old theater and do something good with it—like what you're doing now. It's sat there unused for so many years. I'm glad you got clearance to use it, given its run-down condition. Anyway, I wanted you to know that you've made a difference for her—and for my family. Especially in this season; it's our first Christmas without their dad around."

I swallowed a lemon-size lump in my throat. Though I'd never experienced a *normal* Christmas, I'd written scenes for dozens of them. I knew how they should look and how they should feel. And I knew all about the disappointment that followed when expectations were left hanging on the back of a closed door.

"Merry Christmas to you, Mrs. McDonald."

"You can call me Susie. And merry Christmas to you, too."

☙

At rehearsal that afternoon, Misty had to repeat her questions a dozen times before my brain could actually compute them—a surefire bet my mind was preoccupied. I'm sure she assumed it was because Weston had taken the day off to go visit Savannah in Portland, and I didn't bother to inform her otherwise. But I wasn't fixated on Weston; I was fixated instead on the words of Susie McDonald.

I watched as Josie moved across the stage with confidence and ease. She was no longer the shy, timid girl who auditioned three weeks prior. Her empty eyes were now filled with an infectious joy.

And then there was Justin, who at first could barely stand onstage without shaking and stumbling through his lines. Weston had spent a lot of time helping him enunciate. Now, he was the first to arrive and the last to leave. He had even walked Nan to her car yesterday.

But the biggest transformation was with Kevin, the boxer-brief-wearing wise-man terrorizer. Over the past week, I'd seen something new in him, too. I realized that every time I praised him for a job well done, his posture changed: his chest puffed out, and he held his head high as if he owned the stage. I wondered how much positive feedback he received at home or in school.

As Nan played "O Holy Night" for the fourth time that day, something shifted inside me, and a new vision began to surface.

∽

Nan hooked an arm around my shoulders as we watched the kids leave one by one.

"You've got that deep-thinkin' look about you today."

I let out a soft chuckle. "I have a deep-thinkin' look?"

"Oh, yes, your mother has one, too." Her quiet breathing filled the space between us as we watched the last of the students climb into their cars and pull out of the lot.

"Nan?"

"Hmm?"

"What was she like as a teenager?"

Her heavily loaded sigh caused a twinge of sorrow to prick my heart as I waited for her answer. I may have lost my mom to a new life that didn't have room for me, but she had lost her daughter long before that.

"Your mother was always looking for a place to belong."

The numbness inside my chest expanded to my shoulders, arms, and hands, leaving my fingertips tingling. *Hadn't I always wanted the same thing?*

Nan continued, "Some people are born with a restlessness inside them that is never satisfied. No matter how much they are loved or provided for, nothing ever feels like enough. Summer had so much drive, so much ambition, but when she started focusing too much on what lay ahead, she missed out on everything that was right in front of her."

Nan glanced at me, her eyes filled with compassion. And I knew she wanted me to understand something important—something about the past, something about how although my mom and I were wired the same, my future could be different. *I could be different.* Though the ultimate message wasn't entirely clear to me yet, one thing was.

Summer Cole hadn't left only me.

She'd left Nan, too.

And her absence had stained us both.

"She had a lot of dreams, then, when she was young?" The question strained from my throat.

"Yes, she had big dreams—all of which included a future outside this town. She was gonna leave Lenox right after graduation, but—"

"But then she got pregnant before she could finish out her senior year."

Nan stroked my arm. "And I wouldn't trade you for a million vintage cookbooks."

I laid my head on her shoulder. "I love you, Nan."

She kissed my hair. "Not nearly as much as I love you."

"You can't say that. There's no way to measure it."

"Sweetie, I have decades on you. I'm quite seasoned in the art of love."

Yes, you are, Nan. Yes, you are.

എ

"Wait—are you serious? *The* Weston? The guy who totally humiliated you in front of your entire town?" Cara's high-pitched shriek could've broken a windshield.

"Yeah, the same one, only it turns out he didn't actually do that. I was blaming the wrong person all this time."

"Um . . . wow. I'm totally shocked. So what are you two? Like . . . dating?"

"I'm not exactly sure." *Friends who kiss? Is that a thing?*

"It's not that hard of a question, G. You're either going on dates with him, stealing midnight kisses, feeling butterflies when he's near you . . . or you're not."

"Um . . ."

"*Oh my gosh!* I haven't been able to get you to go on a date for over a year, and then you go home to your Little-House-on-the-Prairie town and *bam!*"

I laughed as I unlocked the door to the theater. It was quiet, dark, and completely empty.

"Well, he's not an easy guy to say no to."

She sighed like a princess dreaming of her prince. "Do you think he loves you, Georgia?"

I nearly dropped the phone as I groped the wall for a light switch. "What? No, he doesn't *love* me! Don't be crazy. We haven't seen each other for seven years!"

"But he's known you your whole life?"

"Well, yeah."

"And he wouldn't let you give him the cold shoulder like you do every guy here?"

"Well, no."

"And he doesn't care that you're the Holiday Goddess?"

I rolled my eyes. "Cara."

"Oh my gosh, he *loves* you!"

"Okay, I'm officially never talking to you about him again."

"Him who?" a deep voice asked behind me.

I jumped, screamed, and threw my phone to the ground—all within half a second.

Weston put his hands up. "I'm sorry . . . I thought you heard me come in." He went to retrieve my phone, flicking on the theater lights in the process.

My hand was still gripping my chest when I started breathing again.

"Hello?" Weston pressed my phone to his ear.

Oh no. "Give me that."

Weston turned around, blocking my futile attempts to knock my phone from his hand.

"Yes, this is Weston. Who's this?"

This is not going to end well.

"Ah yes . . . Cara—Georgia's ever-faithful roommate, right? Yes . . . Well, she's told me a few things about you as well."

I grimaced as he flashed an evil grin.

"Oh, really? That is *very* interesting. I'll have to keep that in mind."

I will kill her.

"Oh, well, hang on." Weston grabbed me around the waist, extended my phone in front of us, and snapped a selfie. Then he proceeded to *send* it to her!

"Weston! Are you crazy?" I smacked his shoulder repeatedly.

"Sorry, Cara, *someone* is being quite needy at the moment. I think I might have to take a rain check on the rest of this conversation. All right . . . will do. Bye."

Weston hung up the phone and offered it to me as if all were perfectly normal.

"You are incorrigible."

"Incorrigible? News flash, this is no longer the 1850s, sweetheart." His face lit with a smile as he gripped my shoulders. "So, what are you doing over here so late? I saw your car on my way home."

"I . . . um . . ."

He raised his eyebrows in renewed interest. "You meeting someone? Perhaps a rendezvous with an old stagehand from the past?"

"No, I just had an idea is all." I strolled toward the stage, touching the worn fabric of the seats as I made my way to the front.

"What sort of idea?"

I bit my lip, hesitating. It might sound insane if I said it out loud.

"How long ago was the drama program cut?" I asked.

"Um . . . it was cut from most of the school districts in the state about four years ago. Why? What's this about?"

"Nothing yet, I'm just thinking."

He threaded his way through the seats to where I stood looking around the room.

"How much work would it take to renovate this building?"

"*This* building?" Weston asked. He seemed taken aback for a moment.

I nodded.

"Well, it needs a new roof, updated bathrooms, and there are some places where the floors are close to rotting out." He crossed his arms over his chest. "Why?"

"I'm . . ." I shook my head. "It sounds crazy."

"You're in good company, then. Say it."

"What if . . . what if there was someone who could do something with this old theater? Make it great again? Bring a passion back to the arts? Not just something for Lenox, but for the surrounding communities, too." I spun in a circle, taking it all in. "It just sits here, Wes. And Josie's mom said it's been on the market for several years."

"Yeah, it has." His words were careful, hesitant even, but my pulse was like a runaway stallion.

"What if *I* could do that? What if *I* could be that person?"

Weston's mouth fell open, and shock veiled his handsome face.

"Maybe it's not even possible." I shook my head as something like a giggle raced up my throat. "Tell me it's crazy, Weston. I mean, I already have a career—a *successful* career—but this . . . I don't know, this just feels *right* somehow."

"You're not crazy, Georgia." He seemed to be measuring his words, but his eyes gleamed with tenderness.

He held my hand, intertwining our fingers, as I looked around the room, visualizing the updates and repairs. I could easily imagine the plays and performances, recitals and readings, but most of all, I could see the faces that walked through the lobby doors.

Faces looking for a place to belong.

CHAPTER TWELVE

December 14—otherwise known as "practice-free Saturday"—was upon us.

I climbed into Weston's truck in my borrowed snow gear—*thank you, Misty*—and a thrill of childish excitement rushed through my veins. I hadn't been tubing for nearly a decade. I looked up at the mountain ahead of us; another layer of fresh snow slept atop it.

"We should probably head home by early afternoon," Weston said, shutting his door. "They say the storm is headed our way late this evening."

I chuckled and clicked my seat belt. "I've heard that for three days now. And last night I finally broke down and ate the stash of Cocoa Puffs I'd been saving for this big storm."

"Well, as much as I'd love to get stuck in a snowstorm with you, I'd like to make sure that you and Nan are well secured tonight in a warm house, with or without Cocoa Puffs."

Tilting my head to the side, I grinned at him. "Thanks, by the way, for carrying in all that wood for the stove. I worry about her doing that by herself when I go home."

"Then don't."

"Don't what?"

"Leave." Weston took my hand and kissed the top of it.

A fluttering erupted inside me.

"Oh, guess what I found out last night? You'll never believe it!" I nearly jumped out of my seat as I remembered my online discoveries the night before.

"What?" Weston mocked me by bouncing in his seat. "Please tell me before you combust."

"Nan knows the realtor who listed the theater. She called him this morning, and he said I definitely have a chance, Weston. There's been no offers on it in a year! I can't help but feel like it's some sort of sign. I mean, seriously, how cool is *that*?"

I couldn't help but notice the skeptical flicker of emotion on Weston's face. "So you've talked to your agent in LA about all this? And she doesn't have any objections to you writing from Oregon if you get the theater?"

"Well, I wouldn't say that exactly. She has some concerns, but . . ."

I also couldn't ignore the way Weston rubbed the back of his neck anxiously.

Not exactly the response I was hoping for. Wasn't he just asking me to stay?

"Why are you acting like that?" I asked.

"Like what?"

"Like you don't care—like I just told you I wanted to purchase a goldfish and not the town's community theater."

"I *do* care. It's just—"

"Just what?"

He gripped the steering wheel. "Remodeling that theater will be a lot of work, Georgia. Don't get me wrong, I want you in Lenox . . . but I also want to make sure you're prepared for that kind of commitment."

Which commitment is he talking about? The commitment to the theater . . . or to him?

I couldn't deny the hurt that seeped into my heart when I heard his words. I'd daydreamed about us working together on the theater—at least in some capacity.

"Okay," I said.

"Georgia, don't do that."

"Do what?"

"That stupid girl-thing where you pretend you're fine when you're obviously not."

"I'm not pretending." *Great, now I'm pretending and lying.*

"I just don't want you to have unrealistic expectations."

I turned my head to stare out the window as the snow started to fall on the pass. We were thirty minutes from the mountain, but the closer we got, the more I felt like going back to Nan's and crying into my pillow . . . not sliding down the bunny slope in a giant rubber tube.

"Georgia?" Weston's soft voice tugged at the wound in my chest.

I couldn't answer him, not without shedding unwanted tears.

"I admire your passion and ambition, I always have. I just . . . I want you to be aware of all that's involved in this decision."

Several minutes of torturous silence lingered between us. His words rolled round and round inside my head on a mental spin cycle, tossing around an insecurity so deep, so tender, that I struggled to push it aside. Though I'd been the one to apply the brakes after Weston stated his feelings—requesting that our new relationship move at a slow pace—purchasing the theater would stomp on the accelerator with a lead foot.

But maybe . . . maybe Weston didn't want to move that fast. Maybe the hesitancy I'd felt from him had less to do with the theater and the work it involved and more to do with *us*.

With me.

115

My throat tightened with a familiar uneasiness. "I realize we've made no commitments to each other. I mean, I was only supposed to be here for a few weeks—it's not like you signed up for anything long-term." I exhaled and picked at the hangnail on my thumb. "Nan is reason enough for me to stay and take this project on. So, please understand, I have no expectations for you if you don't want to be part of this." *Or me.* But somehow I couldn't bring myself to say those words.

Weston remained quiet until we pulled into the white-blanketed parking lot of the ski area. The consistent clenching of his jaw ticked like Nan's piano metronome.

The second he parked, he jumped out of the truck and slammed the door.

Um . . . this could be the worst date in history. No wonder he never made it to date number three.

I jumped out of the truck after him.

As my boots sunk into the snow, I watched him lean over his tailgate. And when he glanced up, the pain in his eyes caught me off guard.

"No expectations?" His staccato words were smothered in hurt.

He pushed away from his truck and trudged back toward me, snow crunching beneath his boots with each step.

"I wasn't talking about *us*, Georgia." He stood inches away from me, his breath crystalizing in the cold air as he spoke. "I was referring to this life-altering project you want to take on." He clamped his mouth shut and pulled at the back of his neck with both hands as I stood staring at him, dumbfounded.

"How could you think I only wanted some sort of winter-break romance with you?"

"I . . . I just thought—"

He reached for my hips and pulled me toward him, his breath tickling my mouth as he spoke. "Stop it. *Please.*" He shook his head and leaned his forehead against mine. "Stop thinking so much. Stop telling yourself that what I feel for you isn't real. Because it is, Georgia. There are so many things I want to say to you, but I can't because you're not ready to hear them. Not yet." Weston's deep breaths warmed my face.

My body was limp with an emotion I couldn't quite identify. Weston let go of me and took a step back, giving me space that I neither needed nor wanted at that moment.

"Why not?" I asked, the snow falling harder, making small piles on my shoulders, hood, and boots.

He studied my face and shook his head as a snowflake landed on his cheek and melted instantaneously. "Because you don't trust me."

I forced my next words out, hoping I believed them. "Yes, I do."

"Do you?" he asked, his eyebrows pulling together. "Then stop worrying about having too many expectations for me—stop wondering if my feelings for you are going to last."

Had he been reading the script written on my soul?

"I care about you, Georgia." His breathy whisper cut through my many layers of self-preservation and doubt.

Tears blurred my vision, and he reached for me again, his cool gloves brushing against my cheeks.

"I want to believe that." And I did.

"Good, because someday I won't be able to hold back what I really want to say."

His lips covered mine a second later. And our kiss opened up a rhythm inside me that I wasn't sure existed until now.

Something was happening to me . . . something as achingly wonderful as it was devastatingly uncertain.

I was falling in love with Weston James.

For the second time.

❦

Despite the intense start to the day, tubing proved to be the stress reliever we both needed. We'd ridden the lift to the top of the tubing hill a dozen times, but my legs ached from the little bit of snow-walking we'd done—and from the fact that I was completely out of shape.

Cara would be griping at me right now for my lack of endurance.

Weston warmed my frozen cheek with a kiss as we rode up the side of the mountain.

"Remember that time we came up here with the youth group? I think it was sophomore year?"

"It was. That was my last time here."

"Are you serious? Willa and I came up here at least ten times a winter. Our parents love to ski."

I smiled and shrugged. "Nan's not a big fan of snow."

"Your mom, either?"

I shook my head. "Nah." *Actually, she wasn't a fan of much—until she met Brad, anyway.*

Weston squeezed me closer to him, not commenting.

"I love it, though," I said, dreamily.

"Love what?"

"The mountains. Sometimes I think it's easier for God to hear us from way up here."

Weston kissed my temple as the ski lift came to a stop. "I think He hears you just fine, Georgia. Whether you're on the beaches of California or in the Himalayas. He hears you."

I grinned at him, my chest exploding with a kind of satisfaction I hadn't felt in . . . maybe forever.

We hopped off the lift, and Weston dragged our tubes alongside him. As I watched his caveman-like stride, I caught a dose of the giggles. A big dose.

"What's so funny back there?" He stopped his trek and turned.

"You look like you're dragging a dead animal behind you after a hunt."

Before I could blink, my back was flat against the snow, and Weston was standing over me, gloating like a third grader who won in a game of Red Rover. *Had he really just pushed me?*

"I may be small town, sweetheart, but I can hold my own pretty well . . . Wouldn't you agree?"

He held out a giant gloved hand to me, but I had no intention of getting up. If I was going down, so was he. As I faked a hold on him, I swept my leg behind his knee and rolled to the side. He came down hard.

"Did I mention that Cara teaches yoga *and* self-defense?"

Weston army crawled toward me as I squealed and tried to crab walk away from him in the snow. I needed to get away from his path of revenge. *Too late.*

With one quick pounce, Weston wrapped his arms around my legs.

"No! No! No!" I couldn't breathe between my eruptions of giggles.

"You started this, O lover of all things winter."

I tried to wrestle my way out of his grip, but my efforts were futile. As I sunk farther into the fresh layers of powder, large snowflakes fell from the sky, wetting my face.

"Stop . . . wiggling," Weston wheezed.

"Never!"

And then we were rolling . . . rolling . . . rolling.

I heard several people shout at us, but we were a nonstop wheel of snow gear and childhood rivalry. As we separated, I knew exactly what he was going to do. Race me!

I pushed myself to keep rolling, even when the tubing slopes came into view on my right.

I didn't care.

Neither did he.

I wasn't going to be the first to stop.

Neither was he.

Finally, after what felt like an eternity being stuck on the teacup ride at the state fair, we both came to a stop.

We lay on our backs panting as the world spun above us. Weston crawled toward me slowly. He looked as dizzy as I felt.

When he was next to me, his heavy, snow-encrusted arm snaked its way across my midsection.

"Did I win?" he asked, breathlessly.

I closed my eyes, smiling as I tried to control my vertigo.

"I think so."

"Yeah?" he whispered. "What did I win?"

My heart. "I'm not sure you're ready to hear it yet."

Weston's laugh was winded. "Touché. You've always had such a smart little mouth on you, Georgia."

"Yes, but you like it."

"Mmm. That I do," he said. "That I do."

When his mouth crashed onto mine, I knew his goal: to show me just how much he liked it. Unfortunately, our make-out session lasted only as long as it took for the snow in our coats, pants, and boots to start to melt, which wasn't long at all. It turns out that when one rolls down a giant hill of snow, one takes in quite a bit of the stuff.

"Come on, Miss Mistletoe." Weston reached a hand down to me as he stood. "We need to get back to town."

Wet, cold, and completely exhausted, we made it to the bottom of the hill, my smile never fading.

And just maybe it never would.

CHAPTER THIRTEEN

To my utter amazement, the storm came early.

Weston rarely showed signs of nervousness, especially behind the wheel. But when he slowed to a crawl around a tight bend in the road, I could feel the stress radiating from him. A focused silence replaced our banter and jokes. Though it wasn't even four in the afternoon, the sky was an opaque gray mass. The snow was so thick that even the brake lights in front of us were no longer visible.

And we still had twenty miles to go.

Even with chains *and* Weston's superior driving skills, navigation proved difficult. I prayed we'd make it home before dark.

Suddenly, Weston jerked the truck to the right, narrowly missing a car that was stopped in the middle of the road. "What the—"

He maneuvered the truck over to the narrow shoulder on the right.

"Stay here. I need to figure out what's going on. Might be a stalled car."

"I'll come with you."

"No, you won't. Stay here, Georgia. The hazard lights are on, and you're more visible here than you are walking around outside or standing behind that car waiting for someone to plow into us."

Though I didn't want to be left alone, I conceded. His look certainly didn't say, "Let's negotiate on this one."

As Weston blurred into the ominous wall of snow, I slipped my cell phone out of my satchel to call Nan.

No signal. *Urgh!*

I counted the seconds until the windshield was completely covered with snow, a solid screen of white. *Fourteen seconds.* I flicked the wipers on to clear it away. And then I started counting again.

Eleven minutes passed before Weston returned, the tip of his nose rosy from the cold.

He slammed the door. "Bad news."

"What?"

"It's not a stalled car. It's an entire lineup of cars. I talked to a driver a ways up—before he lost reception, he got a text saying there was a major accident near the exit for Lenox. Do you have coverage?"

I shook my head. "No, I already tried."

Weston exhaled and rubbed his temples. "I'm sorry about this, Georgia."

"It's not your fault. It's weather—it's fickle."

"Yeah, but I knew it was coming. It's probably going to be a few hours until we can make it home at this point. I haven't seen any plows out yet."

I watched the blades of the wipers as they scraped against the windshield.

"If there was a closer exit, I'd pull off, but you know as well as I do, there's nothing. I'm guessing they'll close the pass to oncoming traffic if they haven't already. When this all freezes tonight, it's gonna be a huge mess."

I bit the corner of my lip.

"You thinking about Nan?"

"Yeah, I've just always hated the idea of her being alone during winter storms."

Weston's chuckle rumbled low, blending with the muted sound of the engine. "That town treats Nan like a queen. She's far from alone, I can assure you of that."

He was right. Most likely, her phone was already ringing with neighbors checking up on her to make sure she'd stocked up on supplies.

I reached behind my seat. "Well, it's a good thing I snatched this giant container of Nan's cookies from the counter before we left."

Weston pulled onto the road again, keeping his hazard lights on. "Yeah, those might end up being dinner *and* breakfast."

My laugh faded the second I realized he could be right.

୧

An hour and a half and approximately two car-lengths later, our hope to make it home before the sky completely blackened vanished as frigid wind gusts continued to pummel Weston's truck.

The only contrast to the darkness that enveloped us was the falling snowflakes caught in the glow of the headlights.

We'd already played a riveting game of Would You Rather?—which, of course, was filled with the most absurd and ridiculous scenarios—and then we tried to guess the story of the family in front of us because the two dark-haired children in the backseat continually turned and waved to us.

And then I had a thought. "I wonder if they're hungry."

Weston glanced down at the cookie container on my lap, and we exchanged a knowing look. "You want to be the Cookie Santa?"

"No, I want *us* to be."

The twinkle in his eye filled my chest with warmth.

We put on our gloves, hats, and scarves as if we were about to trek across the Alaskan tundra instead of a single car-length.

As we approached the vehicle, the driver rolled down his window. There was a look of quiet apprehension etched into his features.

"Hi," I said. "We couldn't help but notice your kiddos in the backseat, and we wondered if we could share some cookies with you all? My grandma made them for us last night."

Weston's hand pressed on my lower back as I spoke, and the gesture warmed me from the inside out.

The woman in the passenger seat leaned over her husband's lap and smiled at us through his open window. "How sweet of you! We'd love some."

"Yeah! We're starving!" One of the kids in back exclaimed, a double gap in his smile where his front teeth had been.

"What you mean to say, Cooper, is *thank you*," the woman scolded.

"Yes, thank you," he echoed immediately.

The little girl next to him nodded excitedly and reached for two cookies. Both parents took a few as well.

"Merry Christmas to you all," Weston said. But as we started to turn back, the doors of an SUV opened and a couple of guys headed toward us.

"Hey . . . are those cookies you're handing out?"

I smiled up at Weston and shrugged.

"Sure are. Would you like some?"

"Yes, thank you! We've been up at Mount Bachelor skiing all day—thought we would grab dinner on our way home, but it doesn't look like that's gonna happen."

Weston shook the driver's hand and held out the container of Nan's oatmeal-raisin cookies to them both. They grabbed several each, and I couldn't help but feel a sense of pride. Nan would be overjoyed.

"Merry Christmas!" we called after them.

As we passed the family in the car again, we heard a familiar sound: *Christmas music.* They had tuned into the nonstop Christmas music station, cracking their windows to release the sound into the snowy mountainside. The lyrics to "Silent Night" rang out crystal clear. The ski guys in front of them tuned into the station as well, the sound pouring from their open windows and sunroof.

And then the car in front of *them* turned on the Christmas music—the trend had caught on quickly.

Once we got back in the truck, Weston tuned in as well. With the windows open, the symphony of Christmas was everywhere.

I inhaled a sharp breath as my soul stirred in a way it hadn't in years. Even Weston was quiet, experiencing a similar attitude of reverence. As the song continued, the volume intensified. Though there was no way of knowing just how many vehicles were participating in this spontaneous outpouring of Christmas spirit, in my imagination there were thousands of cars. Weston took my hand in his, and together we listened, tears gathering in my eyes as I soaked in the sound of wonderment.

"Does this beat your Holiday Goddess clichés?"

I nodded in response, because the truth was, that it did. By miles.

Weston shifted his body toward me, his attention shifting with it. "How did you spend Christmas as a kid?"

"Well, Christmas as a kid wasn't anything like my screenplays, if that's what you're asking."

Weston's head bobbed slowly, his eyes alight with understanding. "I'm not asking about your screenplays. I'm asking about *you.*"

Even with the window open, the air grew stuffy—claustrophobic even. I unwrapped my scarf and pawed at the frayed ends. "My granddad died when I was a toddler. I don't remember him, but Nan says he had a strong faith and a big heart—one that simply gave out too soon. He *loved* Christmastime. He'd dress up as the town Santa and give presents to children." I glanced up at Weston, who was staring at me intently. "Nan took his spirit of giving very seriously, but she made a point to teach me that one should be generous all-year-round, not just during the holiday season. For that reason, we didn't—and still don't—participate in gift giving on Christmas Day. Instead, we volunteered at shelters, baked cookies to give away, and helped families in need." I realized how selfish I sounded. "But I'm not complaining about that—"

"I don't need a disclaimer, Georgia. Go on. What about your mom?"

"Um . . . my mom." The truth was a thickening mass that I couldn't swallow away. He rolled up the windows then and waited.

"She didn't usually spend Christmas with us."

Weston's frown armed my defenses. "What do you mean?"

I squirmed in my seat, wrapping a loose thread around my finger. "What I mean . . . is that she worked really hard to keep me on task during the school year. She felt it was her job to push me academically. But when I had breaks, she took breaks, too." *Okay, maybe that didn't sound as normal as I wanted it to.*

"Took breaks?" Weston questioned.

I nodded, licking my chapped lips.

"You mean, from you?"

My hands tingled with unease. "She knew I had Nan."

Though Weston refrained from saying more, the tension in his shoulders and face was enough to make me want to jump out of the truck. I'd never had this conversation with anyone. It was as impossible to articulate as it was to understand. My mom wasn't abusive or neglectful, she wasn't mean or menacing . . . She was just my mom.

"But you are *her* daughter, Georgia."

The words chafed my heart, rubbing it raw.

A short horn blast startled us both, and a line of brake lights suddenly illuminated a path of movement before us. Weston huffed, released my hand, and put the truck in motion. We rolled forward slowly, tires crunching against the freshly fallen snow beneath us.

Though I hadn't said much, I wanted to retract every word. My pulse quickened as I replayed the conversation again and again in my mind, searching for a missing link that could solve whatever misunderstanding stood between my interpretation of the past and a better, less pathetic version.

But another voice drowned out my own. *"Sympathy never makes us stronger, Georgia. Stop feeling sorry for yourself, and start focusing on how not to make the same mistakes I did."*

I couldn't help but think *I* was the mistake she spoke of. The thing that held her back, inhibited her future, preyed on her weakness.

Several miles later, after the speedometer finally registered our slow pace, Weston spoke.

"What aren't you saying?" he asked.

This conversation was beginning to feel like a fresh hangnail—equally as painful as it was annoying. "Nothing. She's happily married now, living in Florida with her family."

"With *your* family, you mean."

"Right, that's what I mean."

When Weston's eyebrows creased with understanding, my temples began to throb as I prepared for my deepest hurt to be exposed.

But he said nothing.

Lifting my hand, Weston laced his fingers through mine once more, and my fear was quieted, blanketed with relief.

CHAPTER FOURTEEN

The wind howled down Nan's darkened street as we crept toward her house. No lights were on. Anywhere.

Though it was only eight in the evening, the blackout gave Lenox an eerie, post-apocalyptic feel.

On the way home, I'd had spotty cell coverage and never managed to reach Nan. As we pulled up to the house, I finally released the breath I'd been holding.

A frozen wind gust whipped my ponytail violently as Weston took my arm and led me toward her front porch. I tried the door and then knocked. No one answered. I tried again—harder. The wind was so loud she might not have heard me. No answer.

"Do you have your key?" Weston asked.

Frigid cold seeped through every layer of my clothing. I bent and lifted the doormat, revealing the old key. Weston took it from my shaky hands and slid it in the lock with ease, pushing the door open a second later.

No light. No noise. No sign of Nan.

"Weston?" A fog of panic began to cloud all of my senses at once.

"Where are the flashlights?"

I walked toward the kitchen, realizing for the first time that there was no heat coming from the wood-burning stove.

Nan, where are you?

I bumped a dining room chair and nearly collided with the table, when Weston's hands gripped my waist to steady me.

His soothing voice sent chills down my spine. "Careful, Georgia. Let your eyes adjust a bit more."

I put my hands out in front of me and grasped the countertop. Nan always kept a flashlight charging in the corner. *Here it is.* Searching for the switch, I fumbled before finally—

Click.

The entire room was illuminated in an instant.

We saw it at the same time: a note.

Weston reached it first and held it up to the light as our heads huddled together.

G,
At Eddy's house.
Franklin had another episode today. She needed me.
I tried to stoke the fire for you. Please call me as soon as you get in.
Nan

I exhaled and leaned my head against Weston's chest.

"She's okay, Georgia." He kissed the top of my head. "Try your phone again, and see if your call goes through now. I'm gonna start the fire and check in with my folks. I'm glad Willa and Vannie aren't coming home till next week."

I nodded my head in agreement, the knotted muscles across my back slowly starting to release. As soon as I heard her voice, my nerves relaxed. I bit my lip to keep the tears at bay when she told me of the day's events: Eddy making her infamous "storm chili" that tasted like a hot mud bath, and Franklin forgetting to turn off the sink again, which flooded the bathroom.

"Did you kids have fun at the mountain? I worried about you getting home in that awful weather, but then I figured if there was any trouble, you two would just pull off the road and start necking."

"Nan!"

"Well, honey, I might be old, but I know about snow kisses."

So did I. I could remember a recent one quite clearly.

"I think you should stay there tonight, Nan. I'll be fine here once the fire gets going."

"Oh heavens! Did it go out? Georgia, I'm so sorry!"

"Nan, I'm a big girl. I'll be okay."

"Is your beau there? Put him on the phone."

I rolled my eyes. "Nan."

"Don't sass me. Put him on."

Weston crouched in front of the open stove, adding more wood to the crackling fire. His striking features glowed in the light of the flames as I made my way over to him.

"Here."

I held the phone out to him without further instruction, but his grin indicated he knew what Nan was going to tell him.

After a few pleasant exchanges, Weston listened, gave a couple of short replies, said good-bye, and hung up.

"What did she say?"

He laughed and wrapped his arms around me. "She said you should stop being so uptight."

"That's not what she said."

He brushed my temple with his lips. "She told me that I wasn't to leave here without making sure you were going to stay warm for the night—and then she told me where her secret snack collection is . . . since someone already ate through her box of storm Cocoa Puffs."

I rested my head on his shoulder as he kneaded my back with his strong fingers.

"So . . . you want me to stick around for a while tonight?"

More than anything. "Hmm . . . well, we've already had one scandalous sleepover in the not-so-distant past. I don't know if we should push our luck. It's a small town." My smile curved with mischief as our eyes met.

Weston's throaty laugh caused my heart to cartwheel. "Then let's not sleep. Show me where the candles are, and we'll stay up, keep the fire going, listen to the wind, and *talk*. I'll be a perfect gentleman." He kissed the tip of my nose. "I promise."

"This is turning into the longest date in history."

"Correction—this is turning into the *best* date in history."

"I think it should count for dates three, four, and five."

Weston pulled me in closer and whispered huskily into my ear, "I think we should just stop counting."

॰॰

Through the glow of ten votive candles and one heavy-duty flashlight, Weston and I chowed down on Nan's secret stash of sugar. It was snowing hard again. We sat on the floor, legs outstretched, backs against the couch, each with a ratty afghan across our laps, as we watched the flakes fall.

It was past three in the morning, but being with Weston invigorated me. My head rested against his shoulder. He lifted our connected hands to his mouth and kissed my fingertips, each gentle caress singing through me like a personal melody.

"I used to watch you at the park. From my bedroom window," he said.

I tilted my chin, meeting his gaze momentarily.

"I always wondered what went on in that head of yours." He chuckled. "Although now I'm convinced you were plotting screenplays under that old oak tree, while the rest of us struggled to complete our math story problems."

I suppressed a yawn and nuzzled into his shoulder. "You never struggled in school. You got straight As—always had the right answers to your story problems."

"Not always. There was one story problem I could never figure out . . . a story that kept me awake at night and gnawed at me for years."

Weston's finger traced a pattern onto my open palm, and my pulse skipped.

"We've always been intertwined, Georgia. Our pasts are impossible to separate from one another. It would be like trying to extract salt from the ocean." He shifted his body, and his hand cupped the side of my face, his fingers sliding easily into my hair. "This is the story we were always meant to live."

A shallow sigh escaped my lips. "So . . . you're saying you want me to stay? Even if it means that I buy a run-down theater?"

Weston laughed as he pressed his forehead to mine. "I'm saying whatever I have to do to keep you from leaving, I'll do it."

"I think I like this story."

My words were silenced as he kissed me gently, and my heart was fuller than I could have ever imagined.

And for the first time ever, I doubted the story line I'd loved so much as a young girl.

Maybe Louisa May Alcott *did* get it wrong.

Maybe, just maybe, Jo and Laurie could have been happy together.

℘

Despite our goal to pull an all-nighter watching the fire and talking, we fell asleep sometime in the wee hours of the morning. I was on the couch while Weston slept on the floor next to me, several pillows tucked under his head. It was just after six when the power came on, the light from the kitchen blinding me.

"Weston—Weston, wake up."

He lifted his head and rolled over groggily to face me. "Is it next week yet?"

"What?" I giggled.

"I think I need to sleep for a week."

I nudged his leg with my foot. "No, you need to go home and shower. You have to salt the church parking lot, remember? You told me to wake you if you fell asleep."

"Urgh, right. Okay." Weston rubbed his eyes and then ran a hand through his messy hair. I couldn't help but smile. He was adorable—like a bear cub coming out of hibernation.

He stood and planted a kiss on my head. "Best. Date. Ever."

I yawned. "Agreed."

"I'll see you later this morning at service?"

I nodded, rubbing a kink from my neck.

His eyebrows pinched together. "Be careful on the road this morning. I'm sure the plows were working all night, but it'll still be slick." He shook his head. "Actually, why don't you tell Nan I'll pick her up and bring her here in a bit. I don't feel good about her driving."

I smiled. "Stop it."

"Stop what?" Confusion clouded his eyes.

"Being so wonderful."

He grinned and tipped an imaginary hat before walking out the door.

☙

The church service was small.

Though winter storms were common in the mountains of Oregon, they tended to keep people indoors. My pulse jumped when I noticed Nan's friend Mr. Harvey in attendance. He was the owner of Lenox Community Credit Union. I made my way toward him, brimming with excitement, joy, and—

Am I seriously going to do this? Am I really going to buy a theater?

Just as quickly, my doubts were replaced with peace—an oddly reassuring peace. Even the thought of telling Summer didn't dispel my mysterious sense of calm.

"Mr. Harvey. Hi, I don't know if you remember me, but—"

"You're Nan's granddaughter." His puffy cheeks and bald head glistened under the lights.

"Yes, that's right. I'm Georgia. It's nice to see you again. I was wondering . . . Could I come by the bank tomorrow morning and see about getting a preapproval for a real estate purchase?"

His eyes lit up. "Oh, are you looking to buy a house?"

"Um . . . not exactly. But I'd love to sit down and talk with you about it in detail."

"Sure thing. Can you come by around ten? I would love to help you if I can."

I beamed. "Thank you. Thank you so much."

I spotted Nan talking to Violet, the owner of Sunshine Books, and I remembered the debate about *Little Women* that I'd agreed to a couple of weeks ago. So much had changed since that day in the bookstore.

Violet winked at me.

Okay, maybe you're right, Violet. But the jury's still out.

Pulling my coat closed and wrapping Nan's scarf around my neck, I headed for the exit. Weston was probably helping the elderly cross the slick parking lot. Really, his goodness was annoying at times.

I went outside to see if I could lend some assistance when I was assaulted by the sight of Miss Perfect Teeth talking to my Weston. Again.

My Weston . . . really?

Just go with it.

Fine.

Weston's back was to me, but I heard him clearly. "What I'm saying is, I think you should stick to your original plan, Sydney. You're getting in way over your head. It's too much work."

She pressed a red-tipped finger to his chest. "We're both entrepreneurs, Weston. Hard work doesn't deter us."

"Sydney—" Weston's voice held a warning.

"Weston?" Forgetting the ice rink beneath my feet, I quickened my steps like that of a charging bull.

A second too late, I registered the concern on Weston's face. The world started to spin, and soon I was performing a Mexican hat dance, arms stretched out wide.

"Georgia, be careful!"

Too late. Flat on my backside—once again resembling a woman with bladder control issues—I waited for Weston to reach me.

He stretched his hand out to me as Sydney glared at me and said, "I'll let you know what I decide later, Weston."

As I stood upright, Weston's face was still crumpled in concern for me. "You okay?"

"Aside from my wet butt? Yeah. But what was *that* all about?" I nodded toward Sydney as she carefully navigated the parking lot in spiked heels.

He glanced at Sydney. "Nothing."

"It didn't sound like nothing, Weston."

He massaged his right temple. "I was just trying to give her some advice."

I took in a deep breath, desperately trying to pop the jealousy balloon in my chest that was filling at a rapid rate.

"Hey, Wes, can you assist Mrs. Robertson to her car?" Pastor Herbert called from the church steps.

Weston put his hand on my upper arm and kissed my forehead with cool lips. "Let's talk about this later, okay?"

"Okay."

Then he gave me his signature dimple-popping grin and trotted across the parking lot without a single misstep.

It's nothing.

I can trust him.

But somewhere deep down, the word *nothing* gnawed at me, like hunger pangs in an empty belly.

Chapter Fifteen

The bright yellow star swayed to the left and then to the right.

"A little more to the left I think!"

"Here?" Weston hollered down at me from the rafters.

"Um . . ." I put my hand on my hip, debating.

"Hey, Christmas Diva, I kinda need you to make a decision. Like . . . yesterday."

"Hmm . . . okay, I think it's fine right there."

"Thank you, Lord!"

I couldn't help but grin. We'd been hard at work all evening, carrying in sets and positioning them on stage. And by *we*, I mean Weston and his senior brutes. Tonight was our first rehearsal with everything in place. A feeling of relief and satisfaction swept over me.

Misty nodded in quiet affirmation as we watched the students file onto the stage.

"It looks awesome, Georgia. I still can't believe you pulled this off in less than a month."

"Honestly, I can't either."

ఌ

Mr. Harvey leaned forward in his chair, clicking a fancy pen into action before handing it to me.

"I just need your signature here and here so I can submit this over to our preapproval department. If you're approved for the amount you need, you're free to make an offer with your realtor."

"Thank you, Mr. Harvey. When do you think I'll hear back?"

"Possibly tomorrow. It depends on how bogged down our loan department is. Everyone is trying to tie up loose ends before the holidays."

As I shook his hand and headed for the door, I waited for the familiar rush of panic to grip me in its talons or for my mother's voice to berate me for making such a hasty decision.

But for once, neither came.

✧

"You did *what?*"

I sighed. "I know . . . It sounds crazy."

"Um, no. *Crazy* is wearing suede when there are rain clouds. *Crazy* is playing the nickel slots in Vegas. *Crazy* is what happens on reality TV shows with girls who beg for a rose. *You* are buying a theater!"

"Cara. Honestly. You should be an actress. You are way too dramatic to be locked inside a yoga studio all day."

"Maybe so. But that's beside the point. *What are you thinking?*" She paused a beat. "You're really thinking of moving away?"

There was no mistaking what I heard in her voice: a sense of abandonment. Guilt pulsed through my veins. I loved Cara; she was the closest thing I had to a sister.

"Cara . . . even *if* I get the loan, it will likely be a slow process. This kind of thing doesn't happen quickly." I exhaled. "Something's happened since I've been here, something I didn't expect.

138

I realized . . . I've missed it here. I've missed the mountains and genuine smiles, the slow-paced atmosphere, and I've really missed Nan. Yes, it's a small town, but I can make a dent here. Opening this theater could help a lot of kids who need an artistic outlet. It's hard to explain, but it feels right. I'll still write, of course, but I want to *do* more, and being closer to Nan and Weston—" I pursed my lips together. His name rolled off my tongue so easily now. Like I was always meant to say it.

"But what if . . . what if things don't work out with him, G?"

It was a good question—the kind of question a best friend should ask, yet it caused my stomach to roll with discomfort. "It won't change anything."

"Really?" She huffed. "Believe me, I want it to work out for you two, I really do. But this is a huge purchase. It's a big deal, Georgia. You'll be stuck there—even if the worst-case scenario does happen."

"Don't you think I *know* that? I'm not stupid. I've actually thought a lot about this. I don't need you to be my mom. I just need you to be my friend."

I opened my mouth to apologize, when Cara's voice softened, soothing me over the phone. "You haven't told her yet, have you?"

"No."

She sighed, and I heard every word of reassurance she didn't speak aloud inside it. "I'm on your side, G. No matter what. You know that."

My eyes burned with unshed tears. "I'm sorry . . . I know you are. I love you, Cara."

"I love you, too. Please keep me posted."

Pots and pans clanged in the kitchen as Nan made cookies for the bake sale she had organized to benefit Savannah, who was due home the next evening. Willa had called Weston yesterday with the news. He'd sported a permanent grin for most of the day.

Since school was out for winter break, rehearsals had been switched to daytime, which freed up my evenings to spend with Weston. Tomorrow we were cooking for his sister and Savannah at her house—a welcome-home surprise. Having no siblings of my own, I craved the kind of devotion that seemed to come so easily for Weston. But at the same time, I feared trespassing.

"Georgia, are you off the phone?"

"Yep. I am now."

"Come on in here and help me, would you? I need a couple more hands. I'm trying to make peanut brittle for the sale."

Surrounded by an arsenal of kitchen gadgets, Nan was busy stirring liquid goo in a pot, occasionally checking the temperature with a candy thermometer.

"Get that pan ready with the wax paper, please."

I did as she asked. This was serious business. As Nan poured the peanut-filled lava onto the wax paper, her face glistened. She smoothed the bumps with her red spatula.

"Now, can you turn that left burner on? There's fudge in that pot. Just keep stirring."

I nodded. "Sure thing. Are you still planning on hosting the sale after the play? At the senior center?"

"Yep. I volunteered Eddy to help me."

"Oh, good. How is she . . . I mean, with Franklin?"

Nan's smile was sad. "She's strong. He's had the signs for years now. My guess is he will have to go to a facility within the next few months. He's just getting more and more confused."

The low boil prompted me to quicken the pace of the wooden spoon in my hand. I stared into the mixture, lost in thought.

"No need to attack it, Georgia. It's done nothing wrong."

She reached around me and turned the burner off as I stepped aside to watch her work her magic.

"Sorry."

Nan looked at me after she poured the fudge into the pan to cool. "What's bothering you?"

I shook my head, unsure of how to answer.

"Are you having second thoughts about your theater idea?"

Am I? "I don't think so."

When her eyes bored into mine, I knew she was about to pluck the truth from my soul. It's how she worked—her Nan-vision, I called it.

"Whatever you decide . . . it needs to come from here." She touched her heart. "Not here." She touched her temple, smearing a trail of chocolate onto her cheek. "I may be getting older, Georgia, but I wouldn't want you to make a life decision based on proximity to me. No matter how senile I become."

She took a step toward me and placed her warm hands on my cheeks.

"You're important to me, Nan."

"And you're important to me, too, darlin'. But you living inside God's plan is even more important to me. You can't make this decision for anyone and can't unmake it for anyone, either." She rubbed her thumbs over my pinched eyebrows. "Maybe that's not the advice you want to hear from your old gran, but it's the best advice I know. There's only one place that peace comes from. And it's a commodity I wouldn't trade for anything or anyone."

She pulled me close, her sweet scent filling my nostrils and stirring up the childish feelings I had put to rest a long time ago.

"I do feel that, Nan. Peace, I mean."

"Then don't let anyone take it from you."

There was no need for a name drop. She knew as well as I did that my mother would not care about peace or any other kind of divine revelation.

Success wasn't a feeling for her; it was a formula.

❦

Amazingly, rehearsal ran smoothly—both times. Misty managed the blocking while I listened for lines and cue issues. Between Nan, the crew backstage, and the volunteers for lighting and sound who joined us, we were starting to feel like a full-fledged production team. Josie, my modern-day Mary, even hugged me before she ran out to meet her mom in the parking lot. I couldn't remember a more satisfying feeling. I thought again of the peace Nan spoke of. Every time I checked for its presence, it was there, waiting for me, unshaken by my doubt.

I pulled up to Willa's house, and my insides actually fluttered. Going a day without seeing Weston felt wrong. Her house shared a driveway with their parents'. It was small, but even from the porch, I could feel the inviting warmth that lay just beyond the front door.

It swung open.

"I was hoping that was you." Weston wrapped his arms around me, lifting me off the ground and nuzzling his face into my neck.

"Hi." My voice was shaky and breathless. I was glad I hadn't tried to say more.

As he pulled me inside and closed the door, I smelled something baking.

"Did you cook without me?"

"I may have cheated and stolen one of my mom's frozen casseroles from the freezer."

"Weston—"

He put his finger to my lips. "I need you to help me with something else."

His eyes pleaded for my understanding.

"Fine. Just stop with those eyes already."

He grinned and swept a kiss across my forehead.

"This way. I have everything set up."

I dropped my coat and satchel on a chair and followed Weston down a short hallway and into a bathroom. A stool sat in front of the mirror.

"Um . . . what exactly did you have in mind?"

Weston turned around, holding hair clippers in his hand. I gasped.

"What are those for?"

"You're going to shave my head."

"*What?* Why?"

"I want to do it. For Vannie. Willa said she's having a hard time with her hair loss. So I want us to match for the holidays."

My heart melted into a puddle at my feet. I slumped against the doorjamb, staring at him. *Is he truly this wonderful?*

He pushed the clippers at me again. "Is that okay? You don't have a weird hair phobia that I don't know about, right?"

I shook my head, taking the clippers from his extended hand. *No, but if I did, this would have cured me.*

&

Ten minutes later, I buzzed away the last patch of Weston's hair, watching it curl into a half-moon against the tile floor. Running my hand over the rough texture that remained on his scalp, a hypnotic pull seemed to tighten the invisible cord between us.

Weston had always been striking, but until that moment, until I saw him in such a rare state of vulnerability, it was hard to separate which of his features caused my insides to ache whenever his gaze met mine. But now, there was no doubt.

His eyes.

I glanced away, the walls pressing in on me as I reached for the broom.

His warm hand braceleted my wrist.

My pulse hammered under the pressure of his thumb. His touch both strengthened and weakened me. As the broom slipped from my grasp, he hooked a finger under my chin. Our eyes met, embraced in a silent understanding.

"Thank you for being here tonight. For doing this for me."

My spine tingled as his whispered words fluttered across my cheek.

Gripping my waist, he lifted me up onto the counter, pushing my legs to either side of him. His gaze held steady, focused. I struggled for breath as his fingers ran through my hair. One, two . . . ten seconds passed before his hand brushed against the nape of my neck. And then oxygen ceased to matter at all.

I pulled him close to me, clutching his shirtfront while clinging to this moment in the fear that it could slip away, that he could slip away.

When our mouths finally touched, there was no ravenous greed propelling us, no irrational drive making us forget who we were.

Because for the first time in my life, I *wanted* to remember the details.

The tender awareness of his lips against mine created a perfect symphony of emotion. And with one kiss, Weston had reached deeper into me than anyone before.

I'd been sliding in the wrong direction for years, and something—God, maybe—had finally led me back to home base.

To Lenox, Oregon.

To Weston James.

And I'd fallen wholly, madly, completely in love with him.

A tiny whimper escaped my throat just before he broke contact with my lips. Though his eyes still blazed with hunger, he took one step back and then another.

A full ten seconds of silence spun around us.

"I don't think I'll ever go back to my regular barber again."

I suppressed an anxious giggle.

He cleared his throat. "Um, that being said, I should probably handle the cleanup—alone."

Without need for further explanation, I slid off the countertop and on wobbly legs made my way toward the kitchen. *Alone.*

We needed to add a good thousand feet of space between us if we were going to accomplish anything that night—*other than kissing.*

CHAPTER SIXTEEN

Working alongside Weston in the kitchen as we waited for Willa and Savannah to arrive proved no simple task—not when the spark between us felt hotter than the candles I lit on the dining room table for ambiance. Or the steam rolling off the casserole inside the oven.

It was ten minutes past six when they came through the front door, both looking exhausted.

Willa's eyes welled with tears when she saw the beautifully set table. "Wow, thank you both! We're starving."

Weston knelt before a fragile, beanie-wearing Savannah.

"Where's your hair?" she gasped, running her fingers over his prickly scalp.

Weston's chuckle made my stomach flip. "I thought this was the new style. Was I wrong?"

She grinned and pillowed her head onto his shoulder. "Mom said I'll get hair again . . . maybe for Easter."

"Well, I'm sure your mom's right. But you're still my little princess. A really cool, hat-wearing princess."

After we took their luggage to their bedrooms, it was time to eat. We joined hands, bowed our heads, and blessed the stolen casserole and bread.

I also whipped up some chocolate mousse, Savannah's favorite dessert. She beamed when I placed it in front of her. I was thrilled to see her eating, and by the look of it, Willa was, too.

As I stood to gather the plates, my phone buzzed on the counter. I felt like my organs were fusing when I read the number on the screen.

"Um . . . I've gotta take this."

I made a quick exit out the front door, answering just in time.

"Hello, is this Georgia?"

"Yes—yes this is Georgia." Adrenaline mixed with the bite in the wind made me shiver.

"This is John Harvey from the credit union. I know it's after-hours, but I thought you'd want to know so you can make plans for tomorrow. You've been approved. You can make an offer on the theater."

With a soft whoosh, I expelled the breath I'd been holding. "I'm *approved*?"

"Yes. I'll e-mail you the contact information I have for the realtor. I know him personally, so I'll put in a good word for you. With any luck, you could have a signed offer before Christmas. That theater hasn't had any movement on it in years."

"Thank you, Mr. Harvey."

The call ended just as Weston opened the front door. He narrowed his eyes questioningly as he draped my coat across my shoulders.

"Why do you insist on freezing to death?"

"Weston—"

"I mean, there were other rooms you could have escaped to. But no, you must have some kind of freaky need to shiver and chatter and—"

"I'm approved. I can make an offer on the theater."

Weston's mouth clamped shut.

I laughed and then leaped at him, my coat falling onto the ground. His strong arms snaked around my back, holding me as I buried my face into his neck. I drank in his scent.

"Can you even believe it? He said there's been no activity on it in years. This is *really* happening, Wes. I'm going to buy a theater."

I pushed him away suddenly as the words fully registered inside my brain.

"Oh my gosh. I'm going to *buy a theater!*"

Weston's grip on my waist strengthened. "Whoa, Georgia. Do not faint on this porch," he said, pulling me out of my fuzzy, half-frozen delirium.

Before I could rock back on my heels a second time, Weston forced me into the warmth of Willa's house. He deposited me on the couch with a single kiss to the temple. "Sit here, I need to make a quick call." I could only nod in agreement.

And then Savannah was at my side, dressed in pj's and holding a tattered book in her hand.

"Would you read this to me, Georgia?"

I cleared my throat, hoping it would also clear the fog from my brain.

"Absolutely."

She snuggled into my side while Willa loaded the dishwasher in the kitchen. I felt a bit guilty sitting down while Willa cleaned up, but when her eyes met mine, she winked her approval.

"This is my favorite book. It's about a princess."

"I see that. I'm sure I'll love it, too."

And love it I did. It was a sweet story, filled with happily ever afters, the kind we all hoped would be in Savannah's future. With a scrappy-looking blanket wrapped around her hand, she laid her head on my shoulder. And then I remembered a question I wanted to ask her weeks ago.

"Savannah? Do you remember when I visited you in the hospital? You said you'd always wanted to meet me . . . because of our names?"

She lifted her head and played with my hair.

"Uncle Wes picked my name. When I was in mommy's tummy."

"He did? I didn't know that."

She ran her tiny hands over the ends of my hair, and then she curled a lock around her fingertips.

"But what does that have to do with me?"

The back door slid closed, and Weston sauntered into the living room, breaking Savannah's concentration. In one smooth movement, he swept his niece into his arms. "Come on munchkin, it's time for you to go to bed. Can I tuck you in tonight?"

She nodded, grinning at me before leaving the room.

Willa dried her hands on a towel and slumped down across from me. Her petite body was swallowed up by the old recliner. Exhaustion imprinted her every feature. As I studied her, I realized the kind of beauty Willa Hart possessed would never be found in Hollywood. There was nothing superficial or contrived about it. It was pure and untainted. She was lovely in every sense.

I remembered watching her in school, emulating her speech and mannerisms, envying from afar the kind of natural perfection she possessed.

But here she sat now, a young widow and mother in a fight to save her daughter from the deadly web of cancer.

A thick, bitter taste coated my throat as I tried to swallow.

Her eyes crinkled in the corners as she smiled faintly at me. I prayed she couldn't detect the pity that filled my heart.

"She's right, you know."

"Who? Savannah?"

Willa nodded. "When I lost Chad while I was pregnant, I wasn't in a good place mentally. Daily tasks were nearly impossible, much less thinking about having a baby without my husband. I don't think I could have made it without my family. One night Weston told me he found a name, and I loved it, immediately. But I'll never forget what he said about it." She paused, as if recalling his exact words. "He said that the strongest girl he'd ever known was Georgia Cole . . . and if he could give any gift to his niece, it would be that kind of strength. He said, 'Savannah is a name forever connected to Georgia . . . even if only on a map.' And you know what? My daughter *is* a fighter."

He named his niece after me?

"Um . . . you girls all right in here?"

Weston stood looking at us, his eyes going from one to the other. I wiped at my eyes hastily, and Willa nodded. She pulled a piece of paper from her pocket.

"Would you mind running to the store for me, Wes? I need a few things I forgot to grab when we left the hospital."

"Sure thing." Weston turned to me. "Do you want to stay here or come with me?"

"Actually, I should probably be getting home. I have a few things I need to do."

Weston nodded and grabbed my coat as I hugged Willa good-bye.

"I'll see you at the show, Georgia. We're looking forward to it."

I smiled. "I can't believe dress rehearsal is only two days away."

The weight of Weston's hand warmed the small of my back. As we approached my car, he turned to face me.

We spoke at the same time.

"Georgia—"

"Weston—"

"You first." He rubbed his palm on the back of his neck. I still couldn't get over how good-looking he was, even without hair. He waited for me to speak, but I found it difficult to utter a single word. But I had to. He'd given me so much in the last few weeks. And it was time I said so.

I flattened my hands on his chest, and his fingers hooked into the belt loops of my jeans, tugging me closer. "Thank you, for these past few weeks. I never thought I would feel this from anyone but Nan."

"Feel what?"

"Support . . . without limits or conditions."

Several expressions ranging from adoration to concern to something like weary resolution flickered across Weston's face. "Please don't ever forget that. No matter what happens." He cradled my face in his hands. "You will *always* have my support."

His lips brushed across mine.

And then he was gone, trudging toward his truck.

"Hey . . . didn't you have something you wanted to say?" I called to him.

Even from ten feet away, I saw his hand hover with hesitation over his door handle. His reassuring smile was strangely unconvincing. "Not anymore. Good night, Georgia."

∞

Though the drive to Nan's was short, I was grateful for a few moments of quiet solitude. The prayer on my heart took flight the second I pulled out of Willa's driveway. Tomorrow was a big day. Not only was it the day before dress rehearsal, it was also the day I'd be making an offer on the biggest purchase of my life, and from the sound of it, the theater was as good as mine.

I checked again for the peace I'd felt inside me when I first had the vision of making it into something more—something so much bigger than me. It was still there, calming my fear, doubt, and anxiety.

And then I thought of my mom. It was almost midnight her time, but she was headed to Disney World with her family tomorrow. *Do I send an e-mail? Do I text?* As I sat in the dark driveway of Nan's cottage with the heat blasting, I reached for my phone.

I would send a text.

If she were up, she would call me.

If not, I'd wait till her trip was over to tell her. But by then, there was a good chance I'd be the new owner of Lenox Community Theater.

My phone rang thirty seconds later.

"Hey, I'm sorry it's so late," I said.

"It's fine. I'll be up for a while packing. What's up?"

"Well, um . . . I have something I want to tell you."

"Sounds serious. Oh my goodness! Did your agent call? You're getting a real movie deal, aren't you? Georgia—"

"No. That's not it. I did talk to my agent recently, but not about that. I haven't heard anything back on that script yet."

"Oh." I could feel the disappointment in her voice even from three thousand miles away.

"I don't really know how to say this exactly, so I'll just try my best. This trip to Lenox has changed me, given me a new perspective—a new focus. Helping out at the theater and working with these kids has made me fall in love with the arts again . . . and I haven't felt that in a really long time. I've decided I want to stay here . . . to give back. I can write scripts from anywhere." I took a deep breath of courage. "I was preapproved for a loan, Summer. I'm gonna make an offer on the community theater tomorrow. I want to reopen it for good."

Silence.

"Mom?"

Silence.

"That is the stupidest plan I've ever heard, Georgia."

My heart stopped with a hard thud. "What?"

"I did not raise you to be some small-town girl with no future. You are ambitious, determined. Meant for more than I ever was. Where is this *really* coming from?"

Before I could open my mouth to respond, she seemed to have an epiphany. "Is this about a man? Is it that Weston guy Nan talks about? Please tell me you are not making a life decision for a man!"

"Why not? *You* did!" I clapped my hand over my mouth the second it was out. *Oh my gosh . . .*

"Georgia! I was thirty-one years old when I married Brad."

"And you left me for him, Mom . . . *You left me.*"

"Oh, good grief, you were sixteen! You were going off to college anyway." Her voice intensified. "I stayed in that nowhere town so that you could grow up there, around Nan, what else did you expect from me? That I put my life on hold forever so you'd have some-place to come home to for Christmas? That's not reality, Georgia."

A sob caught in my throat as I pressed my forehead to the steering wheel.

"No, Mom, it never *was* my reality. You're right. I never spent a holiday with you . . . here or elsewhere."

"Georgia, I hadn't the first clue what it meant to be a mom when I had you."

"That doesn't change the fact that you *were* one. You still are. *My mom.* The only one I have."

"Yes, well, I'm telling you that if you stay in that town, if you give up your *future*," she spat the word, "it will be the biggest regret of your life."

Tears trailed down my cheeks.

Just like I was to her.

A regret.

It took several seconds to find the courage to speak again. "Well, I'm doing it. I'm making the offer. I just wanted to let you know."

"Well, don't call me crying when it fails."

Don't worry, I won't.

I hung up the phone and closed my eyes as my tears fell in earnest. If only my faithful Hallmark audience could see me now. Crying in my car. Alone. Five days before Christmas.

Everything I knew about holiday traditions came from TV specials and fictional families who ate ham and fruitcake and opened shiny, bright packages tied with ribbons and bows.

But the truth was as fake as my Holiday Goddess name.

CHAPTER SEVENTEEN

In just twenty-four hours' time, I met with the realtor, signed an offer agreement, and ordered enough food and drinks to feed an army of hormonal teenagers. It was dress rehearsal night, and I welcomed being busy. Staying focused on the play was easier than thinking about the other things that weighed heavily on my mind.

As the students, stagehands, tech team, and makeup mafia filed in at half past four, my nerves buzzed to life. This was it. What I loved most about theater—watching a script come to life before my eyes.

"Um . . . Miss Cole? We have a problem back here!"

Uh-oh.

A handful of townsfolk sat in the audience and strained their necks, trying to get a glimpse of whatever disaster was occurring backstage.

It was Kevin—otherwise known as the Angel Gabriel.

He was squatting in the corner, puking into a garbage can.

"Oh no, is he sick?" I asked Josie.

"Well . . . you could say that, I guess." She gave me a don't-feel-too-sorry-for-him shrug.

"What do you mean?" I closed my eyes briefly. I was afraid I knew exactly what she meant.

"I don't think that Orange Crush he was drinking was just soda."

Kneading my temple, I said, "Go get Mr. James, please."

I knelt down beside Kevin and placed a tentative hand on his upper back. "Kevin, do you need me to call someone?"

He lifted his head as I watched the color drain from his face. "No, please don't, Miss Cole. I was just nervous . . . and I thought maybe—"

"You could calm your nerves by spiking your drink?"

He looked at the floor.

I sighed heavily. "Kevin."

"I know . . . I'm sorry. I haven't had a drink in over a month. It was stupid."

"Yeah, it was," a deep voice said behind us.

Our heads snapped up in unison. Weston stood there, his face stern.

"He knows he made a poor choice. He said he was nervous." The protective edge in my voice sounded more like a mother's than a director's.

Weston's eyes shot daggers at Kevin. "I'll handle this."

"I don't think he—"

"Miss Cole, Kevin is a student of mine. I can take it from here."

My eyebrows pinched together as Weston dared me to argue. Stopping midway through my eye roll, I turned to assess the crowd that had gathered around us.

"Okay, people . . . Let's take our places. Who knows Kevin's lines and can fill in for him tonight?"

"I can."

Every muscle in my back tensed.

Sydney Parker, leader of the makeup mafia, batted her eyelashes at me, waiting with feigned hopefulness. Behind her sweet and seemingly helpful tone, I heard the poisonous drip of venom.

"Um . . ."

"I know his lines. Weston can just help me into the harness, and I'll be fine."

Over my dead body.

"The Angel Gabriel is male," I objected.

"And Mary is supposed to be wearing a robe and riding on a donkey," she bit back.

Touché.

I cut my gaze to Weston, who was ushering Kevin off the stage, and heaved a sigh.

What else could I do?

"Georgia . . . curtain call was ten minutes ago," Misty called to me. "People are getting restless out here."

"Fine. But only for tonight. Kevin will be back for the real deal tomorrow."

Sydney flashed me her Colgate grin. "Sounds perfect. I just want to help."

Sure you do. Like a boa constrictor wants to cuddle.

Misty beckoned me to the stage, her eyes pleading. And it was then I remembered I was expected to open the show. Though there were only fifteen people sitting out front—most of them members of the senior center—my knees turned to gelatin. Weston's kiss may have given me the confidence to stand on the stage without passing out, but *talking* while standing on the stage was a whole different scenario. My heart raced as the tech guy in the back pointed to the microphone. I fumbled with it as the deep whooshing sound in my ears drowned out the melody Nan played on the piano.

"Hello . . . um, I'm Georgia Cole. Welcome to the dress rehearsal for the Lenox Community Theater production of *Modern Mary*."

Am I smiling?

Weston walked back into the theater and stopped at the corner of the stage, watching me. I could practically hear his thoughts from there, urging me to overcome my ridiculous stage fright.

"I hope you enjoy the show and buy some cookies. I mean, tomorrow. I hope you buy some baked goods tomorrow night . . . to benefit Savannah Hart. She has cancer. Okay. Thanks."

With that, I set the microphone down and exited stage left as fast as my wobbly legs could carry me. If there had been any doubt of how awful my little speech was, the pitying look on Weston's face confirmed it when he made his way backstage.

"I think we need to work on your public speaking, babe," he whispered in my ear.

I groaned. My cheeks were so hot I could fry a strip of bacon on them.

He pecked me on the forehead and pointed backstage. I nodded. He was needed in the back, to direct the stage crew.

Urgh. And help Sydney Parker into a harness.

I erased that particular mental image and focused my attention up ahead.

Let the show begin.

∽

With only five stops due to lighting disruptions and three missed lines, the night was a great success. Even Sydney as a last-minute understudy had performed perfectly. And acted almost *normal.* When I saw her chatting and laughing with the students after rehearsal, I swallowed a big wad of pride and headed her way.

"Hey, Sydney?"

"Yes?" She raised a thinly shaped eyebrow.

"Thanks for helping out tonight."

"My pleasure."

I forced a smile and started to turn away when she called my name.

"You know, I'm pretty comfortable on stage. I'd be happy to handle the opening announcements tomorrow evening if that would help you."

I blinked. It was painfully obvious to everyone in this town that I was horrible on stage . . . but Sydney Parker?

"Um . . ."

"I mean, I understand that you've put a lot of time and energy into this play, but if it would free you up to handle other things tomorrow night, then I'd gladly take it over for you. It's no problem at all."

I stared at her, measuring the inflection in her voice, the gleam in her eye, the perfect placement of every blond hair atop her head.

Something didn't feel quite right—

Stop it, Georgia. Anyone can change. Isn't that what Nan is always saying?

"I . . . uh . . . I guess that would be okay."

She grinned and pulled me in for a quick hug. I was so shocked by her display of affection that I almost gagged on her musky perfume.

"See you tomorrow night, Georgia."

"Yeah. See ya."

I watched her leave, the four-inch boot-heels and bedazzled backside making her exit hard to ignore.

Nice or not. Good or bad. Right or wrong. Sydney Parker was my new emcee.

Chapter Eighteen

My phone rang as I walked into the theater. Arms full of thank-you gifts for my cast and crew, I pressed my cell to my ear with my shoulder and held the door open with my foot.

"I can hardly hear you. What did you say?" I asked.

Static and strange, robotic sounds followed.

"News . . . your offer," my realtor said.

"What? You're breaking up."

I dropped the box carrying twenty-eight bags of Christmas candy and faced the parking lot. Pressing my hand to my opposite ear to drown out the surrounding noises, I heard the sickening slam of the theater door at my back.

Oh no!

"Um . . . can you please repeat that? What about my offer?"

I whipped around and tried the door. *Locked.*

"Driving on pass . . . bad signal."

The line went dead.

I threw my head back. *Awesome.* Not only was I still in the dark about my offer, I was locked out of the theater as well. Dressed in a black skirt, tights, and heels, I buttoned my coat and checked the windows. *Why must security be such an important thing to people? Urgh!*

Weston picked up on the first ring. "Hey, you at the theater already?"

My heels clicked the ground in the rhythm of a Celtic dance as I tried to keep warm.

"Sort of."

"What's that sound? And why are you panting?"

"My feet . . . and because I'm locked out."

"What? Where's the key?"

"Inside—thus the reference to being locked out."

He sighed that long, drawn-out sigh of his, and I could imagine the face to match it. "Oh, Georgia."

"Hey! My realtor called, and I was trying to balance boxes of Christmas goodies and listen at the same time—"

"What did he say?" Weston's voice became a taut wire, stretched between two points.

"I don't know. He was driving on the pass. The signal was bad."

"I'll be there in a second. Go wait in your car . . . *please*. I don't want an ice sculpture for a girlfriend."

I laughed. "Fine, but please hurry. The cast will be here in twenty minutes."

Weston pulled into the parking lot six minutes later and jumped out of his truck, crowbar in hand.

"What do you plan to do with that thing?" My heels clipped as I scurried over to him across the frozen parking lot.

Stopping dead in his tracks, he looked me up and down. A wide, mischievous grin appeared on his face.

"Weston?" I waved my hand in front of his face. "I asked you a question."

His eyes danced. "You look gorgeous."

My stomach flipped. "Thank you . . . but why do you need a crowbar?"

"Don't change the subject. I'm not focused on the crowbar right now."

I shook my head as my body tingled. I tried to ignore it. "Well, I kind of *need* you to be focused on the crowbar. We have a play to put on, and we can't get inside the theater, remember?"

He exhaled. "Fine. But later—"

"Later we're making an appearance at Nan's bake sale—the one benefiting your niece."

His eyes cleared, and his focus shifted.

"Okay, let's go break in."

I followed him to a window in the back, still confused as to how he was going to use his apparent tool of choice. Weston stood on the balls of his feet as he shoved the curve of the bar under the lip of the window. Within a second, the seal creaked and popped.

"How did you—"

He winked. "I may have spent a few evenings here in high school. This window doesn't have a latch." Pointing to my heels, he added, "Kick those off, and I'll give you a boost."

"What? No. I'm in tights, Weston. Not to mention a skirt. I can't climb through a window!"

"Well, I'm sorry I forgot my Go-Go-Gadget shoes. I can't exactly jump inside. You're all we've got, babe."

I rolled my eyes and glanced down at my outfit again.

"Here, I'll throw my coat over the sill so it won't snag your . . . uh . . . stockings. Okay?"

"Fine. But don't peek."

He grinned innocently. "Of course not."

I slapped his shoulder. "I mean it, Weston. Keep your eyes down."

"I'll keep them on your pretty legs, okay? Don't completely rob me of the beauty of this moment."

Men. Shaking my head, I placed my stocking foot into Weston's cupped hand.

A minute later, I was climbing through the window, skirt and all.

I should win a prize for this. Seriously.

Once I was inside, Weston tossed my heels up to me and winked.

"I'll meet you at the front, gorgeous."

❧

The murmuring of the crowd heightened my senses.

Breathe, Georgia. Just breathe.

Everything was set. Everyone was in his or her place.

This is it.

Savannah and Willa sat in the front row. When I saw them, my heart took flight. All of it had been worth it. That little girl's smile could melt a glacier. She waved to me as I peeked out from behind the curtain.

And then Sydney took the stage.

"Good evening, everyone. Tonight is a special night for several reasons. Not only are we fund-raising for Lenox's very own Savannah Hart, we are also about to witness a unique rendition of the Christmas story."

Okay, maybe she isn't as bad as I thought.

"Now, as many of you know, there is a bake sale being held at the senior center immediately after the performance, and one hundred percent of the proceeds will go to benefit this great cause."

Sydney turned to glance in my direction, and as she did, a nervous shiver went down my spine.

"But I also wanted to share some very exciting news—since it pertains to this beloved building. Georgia Cole and Weston James, can you join me on the stage?"

What? No . . . What is she doing?

Weston walked onto the stage from the opposite side, looking as surprised as I did. His glare suddenly turned murderous as he focused on Sydney. On shaky legs, I walked forward, reaching Sydney's side as the crowd waited, the air thick with anticipation.

"I am sure that many of us remember the last time this building was used for a production of this magnitude. In fact, these two standing beside me were the original leads that night, until Georgia had a little mishap on stage, and I filled in." Sydney smiled as several of the townspeople chuckled. I could feel the color drain from my face. My pulse whooshed in my ears like crashing ocean waves. Out of the corner of my eye, I saw Weston reach for the microphone, but Sydney took a step forward, leaving us standing behind her. When his hand didn't reach for mine, an icy awareness filled my blood.

"Since that night years ago, this theater has held a very special place in my heart, and as of this afternoon, my offer to buy this building has been accepted. It will undergo some spectacular renovations in order to become Parker Fitness and Spa—Lenox's first health club! And all of it has been designed by our very own Weston James, my business partner."

Whoosh.

Whoosh.

Whoosh.

I blinked several times. Savannah's tender face grounded my urge to run, or cry, or kick someone—or two someones. The stage lights above bore down on my skull as the weak applause from the crowd died down enough to hear the first three notes of a well-known Christmas medley. As soon as Nan struck the keys of the piano, the sound jolted me back. I forced a smile and scurried off toward backstage. My legs felt hollow and numb, each step heavy and deadened by my stupidity and regret.

I gripped the velvet curtain and swayed unsteadily. There was commotion all around me, but I couldn't move. My knees threatened to give out, and the pressure building in my chest made me short of breath.

"Miss Cole! Are you all right?"

Kevin stood in front of me, concern filling his eyes.

Josie touched my shoulder. "Should I go on, Miss Cole? The music started already."

Though my throat was completely dry, I managed to croak out a quiet command.

"Yes, Josie."

I couldn't let go of the curtain that was in my white-knuckle grasp. "Everyone get back to your places. We're starting."

Kevin didn't budge. "Shouldn't I get Mr. Jam—"

"*No.* I mean, please don't, Kevin. We're starting."

He nodded reluctantly and walked away, looking back at me every few seconds before he finally disappeared from view.

Business partner? Designer? Fitness center?

The words were a sledgehammer of pain, striking against my heart repeatedly.

And just like seven years before, the pieces of my life shattered and fell, while Weston James stood back and watched the show.

CHAPTER NINETEEN

Despite the rolling sickness in my gut, I made it through the show, physically shrugging Weston off each of the six times he tried to pull me aside during the performance. I had only so much strength—and right now, I needed it for Savannah.

Not for her backstabbing uncle.

I walked to the lobby to shake hands with the townspeople, to accept flowers, and to encourage patrons to head over to the senior center. All the while my smile felt as plastic as Holiday Barbie's.

The kids had rocked it. And they knew it.

Every moment of every scene had been on target, and they had shone like bright beacons of talent. Especially Josie and Kevin. But instead of brimming with pride, a second wave of grief swept over me. Sydney wasn't just destroying the theater: she was taking away these students' ability to belong to something more. Something that mattered. And though I wanted to weep with pride for all they had accomplished tonight despite their emotionally comatose director, a vine of sorrow coiled around my heart.

Several parents expressed their surprise about Sydney's announcement, but I simply nodded, refusing to comment. I didn't know what to say. I still didn't understand it myself.

Nan and Eddy left for the senior center when the show finished, and I was grateful for that. Hugging Nan would be my undoing, and I needed to stay strong and in control.

As I flicked off the last of the lights for what would likely be the last time, I heard his voice.

"It's not what you think, Georgia. Let me explain."

My laugh was humorless. "Oh? And what do I think? That you lied to me? That you played me? That you sold me out for Sydney Parker?"

"It's not like that, Georgia."

I spun around to face him. "Then tell me what it's like! I guess it wasn't enough for Sydney to be the mastermind behind my most humiliating moment seven years ago. This time she went and got herself an accomplice."

He rubbed his face. "Sydney's not—"

I held up my hand. "You know what? I don't want to listen to this. Whatever sick and twisted relationship you have with that woman is none of my concern. You two are made for each other."

I pushed the door open and stepped outside. He followed me, waiting as I turned the key in the lock.

Even in the darkness, I could see the deep furrow in Weston's brow. "None of your concern? Don't say that, Georgia. Sydney and I don't have a relationship!"

"Excuse me, I guess I should say, *business partner*." I paused, using air quotes for emphasis. "Here, you might want to give this to her." Slapping the key into his palm, I refused to let the threatening surge of emotion fill my chest.

The click of my heels matched the speed of my heart as I raced toward my car, but Weston arrived first.

Urgh.

"Sydney and I *are not* business partners. She contracted me to draw up some plans for her about six months ago, but the city turned down her permit to build—*twice*. When she mentioned the theater—"

I shoved him.

He rocked back, his eyes round with surprise.

"You knew she was going to make an offer, and you listened to me go on and on about my plans without telling me? You're revolting!"

"I was just as surprised as you were tonight! Do you really think I want Sydney to turn that theater into a spa? *Really?*" He shook his head. "Georgia, I didn't want to tell you because I was doing everything in my power to change her mind. I didn't think she would do it."

I glared at him. "Like what?"

He rubbed his head and took a deep breath. "Like paying her back my fee for drawing up her blueprints. And it was more than just a few pennies, believe me."

"No."

"No, *what?*"

"I don't want to believe you."

"Well, it's the truth, Georgia. I never wanted Sydney to buy that theater. I want you here. I want you with me. I want—"

I shook my head. "It was a mistake to think I could stay here. My mom was right."

"Your *mom?*"

Weston grabbed me and forced me to look at him.

"That's it, isn't it?" The unsettling calm in his voice sliced me deeper than the blade of a knife ever could.

I fought against his hold. "Stop it, don't try to psychoanalyze me. This is about *you*."

"No. *This* is about *her*! I'm not trading you in, Georgia. I'm not waiting around for a better deal . . . I'm not giving you up. Not for anything." With one quick yank of a loose emotional thread, he was unraveling me.

"Stop, *please*." I squirmed in his grasp.

"That's what you meant the other night—about feeling *support without condition*. But what you really meant to say was that outside of Nan, you haven't felt *love* without condition, right? That the only time you felt loved by your mother was when you were on top, succeeding and living the life she didn't get to live herself. Well, her life is not yours!"

I shook my head, a sob breaking from my chest.

"Georgia," he whispered.

My chin quivered, my name a lonely, pathetic whisper on his lips. "It's over, Weston."

"I'm not losing you, Georgia—not over this."

"I've never been yours to lose."

His hands fell away, the expression in his eyes punching me hard in the gut.

Do it. Rip the bandage off.

"I don't belong here. And I don't belong with you. Go to the bake sale, they're expecting you, but please don't come after me. I won't change my mind."

His jaw was clenched tight as I got inside my car and pulled the door closed.

And with all the strength I had, I slammed another door closed as well. One I prayed would never be reopened.

Not by the kid who chased me around with a glue stick, not by the man who had stomped on my dreams—and my heart.

∽

Nan offered her condolences over a steaming cup of coffee, after I replayed the realtor's message on my phone. It confirmed what I already knew—that Sydney's bid had been chosen over mine. But I was no longer in the mood to shed tears or feel sorry for myself. I had done enough of that last night on my pillow. I had only one mission.

To finish a debate I had started three weeks ago.

The bells chimed as I stepped inside the bookstore. Violet looked both surprised and pleased to see me.

"Well, I hoped I would see you back in here before Christmas. It was a great show last night. Hope there was a lot of money raised. The place was packed."

I nodded. "Thanks. I don't know the final figures, but I think it will be a good-size check."

Violet pulled her glasses off and studied my face. "You all right?"

"Not exactly, but I do want to have that debate—the one I promised you. About *Little Women*."

Her mouth curled into a half smile. "Sounds like you've put some thought into this."

I swallowed. *Not enough, apparently.* "Yes."

"Okay, then. You start. Tell me why Laurie and Jo were wrong for each other. What did Louisa May Alcott know that we don't?"

Easy. "They were too similar. Hot-tempered, stubborn, passionate. Not to mention there was *way* too much history between them. Sometimes starting over is the best thing we can do for ourselves, and Jo did that with the professor."

"Yes, and he was a bore! Sure, opposites attract, but *sometimes* the only way to understand who we are is to see ourselves through the eyes of someone just like us. Laurie and Jo had an understanding. They had a unique bond—one that is difficult to find in friendship, much less in love. And *history*? Tell me, if you were given the chance to watch the love of your life grow up, share in his memories, learn his family dynamics, wouldn't you take it? No matter when love begins, history is only a step behind us—always."

I bit the insides of my cheeks, thinking. "Then why did Jo turn him down? Why did she say no to his proposal?"

My head throbbed with the quiet tick of the clock.

"Why don't you tell me," said Violet.

I stared at the stain on the carpet. "I don't know."

She chuckled. "Georgia, I've been married to my best friend for thirty-eight years. I've learned a few things about love and regret in that time."

Sliding my gaze up to hers, I watched her lean over the counter as if to tell me a secret. "Fear is love's greatest opposition. Now . . . what are you afraid of?"

The ache in my chest suddenly ignited, singeing the edges of carefully wrapped truths and melting layers of old hurts. "I should get going. Thank you again for the discounted book, Violet."

"Georgia?"

Two steps from the door, I turned. "Yes?"

"I married my Laurie . . . and it was the best decision of my life."

♁

My hair was up, my sweats were on, and I was eating through my second box of Cocoa Puffs. Apparently, I didn't need a storm warning to create a new stockpile.

"Come with me, Georgia. I don't want you to be alone tonight."

"I'm not, Nan. I have Mary Higgins Clark to keep me company."

She scowled. "That doesn't seem like appropriate reading on Christmas Eve."

"Well, *I live* Christmas Eve eleven months out of the year. I'll be fine."

Nan didn't move an inch.

"Go, Nan. Eddy needs you."

Her shoulders sagged with her exhale. "I'm sorry, Georgia."

"You have nothing to be sorry for. You're a good friend. Eddy is lucky to have you, and you're lucky to have her."

I was pulling another handful of cereal from the box when I saw the tears falling from her eyes.

"Not about that." She waved her hand in the air. "About your mother. When your grandpa died . . . a part of me did, too. The holidays became so painful for me. He was the king of tradition and Christmas spirit, so I guess that when your mom acted indifferent toward the whole thing, I was kind of relieved. I just wanted to fill time, to spend the season helping others. But I'm afraid it came at a greater price than I realized. I didn't think enough about the little girl in my own house. I won't make excuses for your mother, Georgia, but whatever part my decisions have played in your hurt . . . I'm truly sorry."

The handful of Cocoa Puffs plinked onto the hardwood as I stumbled to my feet and flung my arms around her. I'd never seen her so exposed or so vulnerable.

"Nan. I could never be upset with you. I don't blame you for anything." Then I squeezed her tighter. "I wish I could stay." I wasn't ready to leave her again.

"I know, darlin'. I know. I wanted that, too."

Nan pressed a kiss to my forehead and made me promise I'd join her at Eddy's if I started to feel lonely. Little did she know that Lonely and I had coexisted inside my world for as long as I could remember. Life was no different on the holidays.

"I'll be back late, but we can do Christmas breakfast together, okay?"

"Okay." I smiled. "But Nan . . . I did get you a gift this year. So you'd better prepare yourself now, all right?"

She shook her head and chuckled. "I suppose."

That was as good as I would get on that particular point, no matter how sentimental she was feeling tonight.

Snuggling into the sofa, I picked up my latest mystery novel and let my eyes drift over the words and paragraphs, pages and chapters. I didn't comprehend a single phrase.

At a quarter to nine, I decided I needed a walk.

I didn't care that it was freezing outside. I layered myself with Nan's scarf and hat, and the warm black gloves Weston had bought me nearly four weeks before.

The streets were silent, but lights glowed in every house. It was Christmas Eve after all. Who wasn't home celebrating with family, reading "The Night Before Christmas," and drinking hot chocolate?

Me.

I tugged my coat tighter and tromped up the frosty knoll toward the park. If there was one place I could imagine allowing myself to get frostbite, it was that park. After all, it was part of the majority of my childhood memories. The town's big blinking Christmas tree was smack-dab in the middle of the open field, but that wasn't the best part of the park this time of year. The Nativity scene, which was displayed a couple hundred feet away, was even more striking. The ground crunched beneath my feet as I made my way toward it.

It was the typical setup: the stable, the manger, the wise men, the shepherds, and, of course, Mary and Joseph. But this time, as I stood staring, it no longer felt typical. I had retold the Christmas story dozens of times—profiting greatly from its themes—yet tonight, it felt . . .

I knelt down in the hay, my heart beating hard and fast.

As I stared into the manger where some child's baby doll lay, I heard Violet's voice sigh through my mind.

"Fear is love's greatest opposition . . . so what are you afraid of?"

"What am I afraid of?" I whispered.

As soon as I asked the question, I heard another voice . . . a stronger voice.

"I'm not trading you in, Georgia. I'm not giving you up."

As my head fell forward, the walls inside me collapsed one by one.

And then my tears came.

Not for the woman I had become, but for the girl I had lost along the way.

For all the years I tried to make up for my mother's regrets with awards, scholarships, and contracts—I never truly believed she would love me without them. Yet someone had.

For twenty-five years Nan had showered me with love and affection, but I'd been too focused on the gaping void my mother left behind, too absorbed with the crater of insecurity she'd created . . . that I didn't see what was right in front of me.

And maybe I'd done the same with Weston.

And with God.

Believing the voice of my fear—both past and present—had not kept me safe from rejection. It had held me hostage.

Lifting my eyes to the manger, I let a sob break loose from my chest. Swaddled inside that wooden crib lay the purest form of Unconditional Love I would ever know.

And if I couldn't accept God's perfect love for me, His sacrifice for my salvation, His divine plan for my life and future, then I would never truly be free.

Neither to receive love nor to give it away in full.

Chapter Twenty

Halfway to Weston's house, I realized whatever romantic notion I had of professing my undying love to him on Christmas Eve may not have been my brightest idea to date. My feet were bricks of ice, and my nose was colder than Frosty's frozen carrot stick. Even with Nan's scarf double-wrapped around my face, every pore tingled.

One more block.

In reality, Weston's house was only a mile from the park, but in near-freezing temperatures that mile felt like ten. Most of the Christmas lights were turned off for the night. Surely, all the children were safely tucked into their beds waiting for Santa Claus to arrive.

As I neared his house, disappointment slowed my steps.

No car.

No lights.

No Weston.

I collapsed onto his front-porch steps and hugged my knees to my chest. *Of course, he wasn't home!* He had a family . . . He was probably stuffing stockings and eating gingerbread right now, or reading to Savannah before he tucked her into bed for the night.

As I stared at the tip of my boots, I saw it: a snowflake. The complex detail of it melted as soon as it made contact with my shoe. My heart lifted at the sight. There were so many amazing and intricate mysteries in the world; I just needed to open my eyes to see them.

Lifting my sappy, tear-filled eyes to the sky above, I stared in wonder as the snow fell. Holding out my gloved hand, I caught snowflake after snowflake in my palm. Suddenly, headlights nearly blinded me. I shielded my eyes with my arm.

"Georgia?" Weston slammed his door and jogged around his truck, slowing as his eyes took me in.

I blinked him into focus, and his expression hardened.

"Um . . . hi."

"What are you doing, Georgia?" Weston's face held a mix of concern and confusion. "It's almost midnight—on Christmas Eve."

I stood, the snow drifting around us. Biting my numb bottom lip, I tried to stop the quivering of my chin, but it was a lost cause.

"I . . . wanted to say . . . some things."

His gaze roamed my face. "You look terrible."

Of all the things I'd expected him to say, that wasn't it.

He glanced down the street and back, shuffling closer. "Tell me you seriously didn't walk here."

"I was . . . already out."

He took my hand and pulled me toward his door, unlocking it with his free hand and pushing it open for me.

So far my romantic stunt was not quite going as planned. I'd pictured running and laughing and kissing and—

"Stand there, you're soaking wet. I need to get you some dry clothes before hypothermia sets in. You look halfway to rigor mortis." He took three steps and then whirled back to face me. "Are you trying to make me crazy?"

Shivering involuntarily, I shook my head.

He left the room and returned a minute later with lounge pants and a hooded sweatshirt. Without another word, I went to the bathroom and changed, catching sight of my bluish-purple lips in the mirror.

Wow . . . I do look awful.

When I walked out of the bathroom, holding the sweatpants at my waist—I'd rolled them three times to keep myself from tripping—he was carrying several large quilts in his arms.

"Sit."

I obeyed.

He tucked the quilts around me like he was folding an overstuffed burrito, and he knelt in front of me.

"Don't you ever do something so careless again, Georgia." He scrubbed his hands over his face. "If you wanted to talk, you should have called. I've been going out of my mind these last two days trying to figure out how to balance giving you space and breaking your stubbornness . . . and then you show up at my house tonight halfway frozen."

"You've been going out of your mind?" I whispered, my heart flipping wildly.

He laid his stocking-capped head in my lap and chuckled. "Yes, Georgia." Snaking his arms behind my back, he hugged me close. "Please tell me you believe me now."

As his eyes lifted to mine, I knew the answer. "Yes. If you tell me that Sydney isn't your business partner, or any other kind of partner . . . I believe you. But I still wish you had told me what she was up to, Weston. About her wanting to make an offer on the theater."

"I know. It was stupid. I really thought I could spare you the worry and convince her otherwise. I should have told you." He kissed my wrist. "I'm sorry."

"I'm sorry, too." I rubbed my hands over his knit hat, the warmth thawing my fingers. "You were right, though."

"About what?"

"Everything—my mom."

Weston touched my cheek. "You have no idea how much I wish I wasn't."

My chest ached at his words. "I've built my adult life around ideas and stories I knew next to nothing about . . . until now. Until you. Only now, I want the real thing, Weston."

The curve of Weston's mouth made my heart pound. Little by little, his dimpled grin became full-blown. "I'm in love with you, Georgia Cole. And I think I always have been." He kissed each of my frozen fingertips. "I see your face in every childhood memory, but I want to see it in every memory that's to come, too. My future was always meant to be connected to yours."

Leaning forward, I took his face in my hands and kissed him. At first it was sweet and sincere, deepening quickly to hungry and wanting. And want him I did. Forever.

"I love you, too, Wes. More than I ever imagined I could love anyone. And even without the theater, I know I belong with you."

His lips found mine again as he made his way onto the sofa.

With hands braced at the nape of my neck tenderly, Weston kissed me and unleashed the passion I'd heard in his words, seen in his eyes, and felt in his touch.

I was loved by Weston James.

When our kiss finally broke, he glanced at the clock. "So . . . it's official then."

"What is?" I giggled.

"Our story has surpassed all your cheesy holiday romance screenplays. We just said 'I love you' for the first time at midnight on Christmas Eve. Doesn't get much better than that."

I swatted his shoulder and pulled him close again. "No . . . and as cliché as it sounds, I wouldn't trade our story for anything in the world."

His eyes sparkled as he kissed me again.

"Merry Christmas, Georgia Cole."

"Merry Christmas, Weston James."

❧

After spending the wee hours of Christmas morning baking several large pans of cinnamon rolls with Nan, I checked off another name from the list of lucky people fortunate enough to receive her heavenly pastries. She changed the list every year, making sure to include widows and widowers, families struggling financially, and those who had recently experienced loss. I admired her for so many reasons, but that morning, the tradition of hers shone even brighter as I reflected on my moments in front of the manger the night before.

I had added both Josie's and Kevin's families to the list. Everyone was beyond grateful as they received the hot plate, hugged me, and wished me a Merry Christmas.

As Nan pulled into the Greenway neighborhood, I glanced up at her.

"Nan? I don't think we have a delivery in this neighborhood."

"Yes. We do."

"Um . . ." I glossed over the list again. "Nope, we really don't."

"It's under J. Parker."

"J. Parker? Is that . . . Sydney's father?"

"Yes." She turned at the next corner, passing several estates decked out in gaudy holiday trimmings.

"But why, Nan?"

Eyes full of empathy, she pulled into a driveway. My stomach bottomed out. Sydney's white SUV was parked in front of the garage.

Nan rested her hand on my knee. "Sometimes we need to love our adversaries more for our sake than for theirs."

"Nan, you don't know—"

"Georgia. I don't care nearly as much about the wrong she's done to you as I do about what your heart chooses to do with it. No one's life is exactly as it seems. Everyone is capable of being redeemed."

That seemed questionable when it came to Sydney Parker.

I stared at my Yoda-like grandmother and thought of every credible argument as to why I wasn't going to get out of this car.

But her expression was steady.

If there was a woman more stubborn than me, it was my Nan.

I grabbed the plastic-wrapped snowman plate filled with buttery goodness and trudged up the driveway as slowly as humanly possible. I noticed then that this was the only house on the street without Christmas lights or a giant inflatable snow globe in the yard.

Hiking up my pants along with my pride, I said a prayer under my breath as I knocked on Sydney Parker's front door.

A man—John Parker I assumed—swung the door open. His disheveled dark hair looked like a peacock's tail after a fight. But his face was handsome, young, with a light scruff around his jaw. There was no doubt he was the father of one Miss Sydney Parker.

"Who are you?" His glassy eyes ticked back and forth rapidly, putting my nerves on edge. There was something off about him, about his voice and the way he stared at me. It was as though he could see something I couldn't.

"I'm—" I shoved the plate toward him. "I'm Nan's—Nancy Cole's granddaughter. These are for you. Merry Christmas."

The man tilted his head, blinked once, and snatched the plate from my hands roughly. "You want money—a delivery fee?"

"Um, no, they're a gift." I started to turn away from the awkward man when I heard—

"Daddy? Who's at the—" Sydney stopped dead in her tracks, her face a canvas of a variety of emotions—going from weary exhaustion to wide-eyed disbelief and then finally revealing a slow-simmering humiliation that pinkened her makeup-free cheeks. She touched her dad's shoulder, and he shrugged her away, the plate of homemade cinnamon rolls slipping out from under the plastic wrap and splattering onto the floor. I sucked in a sharp breath—and resisted the urge to run from this porch and never look back.

"Stupid girl! I haven't paid for those yet!" His brow crumpled in anger.

"Daddy, go wait in the other room, please." Sydney dropped to the floor, scraping up frosting as he stood there rocking back and forth on his feet.

He seemed to consider this for a moment, and then he looked back at me. "You said today's Christmas?"

"It is." My voice squeaked with doubt.

"Daddy . . . *please*. Go wait in your recliner. I'll get your breakfast to you in just a minute."

With one final glance in my direction, he shuffled away, muttering to himself. I suddenly realized why Sydney didn't want to meet with the costume committee in her home. She was hiding her mentally ill father.

Sydney tried to clean up the frosting on the beautiful entryway tile with the edge of the plate, but she ended up just swirling it around in the process. Something inside my chest pulled tight. I didn't like this girl, or the things she'd done to me, but when every instinct told me to turn away from her, I couldn't.

I couldn't leave.

I knelt down beside her, and her eyes flicked to my face.

"What are you still doing here? Go home to your family, Georgia." Her voice caught on the word *family*. It was a word that had snagged my voice plenty of times.

"Do you have any paper towels? I think those might work better."

She stood up without speaking and left the entryway. She was back moments later with a roll of paper towels. I took one from her hand and wiped up the sticky mess without saying a word.

When we were both standing, Sydney's shoulders sagged with the weight of a thousand lifetimes. And something inside me shifted—something that felt less like comparison and more like compassion.

"Let me get you a new plate of rolls. Nan has extras in the car."

She shook her head. "It's okay. He's not supposed to have sugar anyway—it doesn't mix well with his medications."

Oh. "Well . . . um . . . Merry Christmas, Sydney."

The smile that came to my face wasn't my normal forced-for-Sydney-Parker grin. It was instead an authentic, joy-filled smile. And I meant it.

Whatever was going on inside this house, or inside her world, it wasn't easy. It didn't justify what she'd done or make me understand her motivations, but it did make her human.

Just like me.

The door closed with a soft click, and I headed down the driveway toward Nan.

"Georgia?"

I spun back around to see Sydney's pale face staring back at me from a small crack in her front door.

"Yeah?"

"Merry Christmas."

೮౨

That afternoon Weston picked us up to join the Jameses' traditional Christmas dinner. Even though Savannah was still undergoing treatments, there was much to celebrate, like the Christmas pageant fund-raiser and bake sale, which had brought in more than double what we'd expected. Other than the book I planned to give Nan later that night, I hadn't shopped for gifts. But this year, I didn't feel the absence of fancy packages. Every possible hole in my heart had been filled, and I had never loved a Christmas Day more.

Hearing Savannah squeal at the sight of Weston's dollhouse made my heart dance. It was beautiful, and so was she. Willa sat in the far corner and watched her daughter play while I said yet another silent prayer for the little girl's mother. I longed to see her laugh and experience true joy once again.

Placing each piece of tiny doll furniture into Savannah's house was the highlight of my day—that is, until Weston turned to me with mischief in his eyes.

"Georgia Cole . . . are you ready for your Christmas gift?"

"What? But I thought we—"

He held out his hand to cut me off. "Calm down, Miss Holiday Hype. Up until a couple of hours ago I didn't think my present to you would happen. But I guess there is such a thing as a Christmas miracle."

I stood up from my place on the floor with Savannah. "What are you talking about, Weston?" I gulped down the pounding that was lodged somewhere between my ribs and my chin.

In true Weston form, he sauntered toward me with a grin as outrageously wicked as it was glorious. He wrapped his arms around my waist and touched my nose to his.

"What would it take for you to stay here—in Lenox—with me?"

"Weston," I whispered sadly. "We talked about this last night . . . for hours. I have to go back to LA, at least until I figure out—"

"And what if it's figured out?"

"What are you talking about?"

He stared into my eyes, and I gasped. "What did you do?"

"*I* didn't do anything. I'm just the messenger. But I have it on good authority that Sydney Parker rescinded her offer for a certain theater in town. She's decided to wait until she can get a permit to build."

"What? How do you know that?"

"She called me right before you got here and told me to pass the message along to you."

An overwhelming wave of joy washed over me as Nan, Willa, Savannah, and Weston's parents hollered in glee. Tears rolled down my cheeks faster than I could swipe them away.

"I can't believe it." My words were hardly audible through my sobs, but Weston pulled me close and whispered in my ear.

"Believe it, Georgia. You were meant to live here as much as I was meant to love you. Merry Christmas."

Through my tears, I kissed his face over and over again. "I love you, too. Merry Christmas."

ↄ

After leaving a voice mail for my mom wishing her and the family a Merry Christmas, I walked into the living room, where Nan sat.

"I have something for you, Nan."

Her eyes crinkled as she shuffled over to me in her bathrobe and slippers, spiced apple cider in her hand. The party at the Jameses had wound down around nine. We'd just gotten back to her cottage.

"You know how I feel about gifts, Georgia."

"And you know that I warned you, so sit down." I patted the couch cushion beside me.

"What a bossy little thing you've become."

She sank down beside me, and I laid the package in her lap.

"Open it, Nan. It won't bite you."

After placing her cider on the side table, she leaned forward and carefully tore the paper away. Her hand moved to her face as she gasped.

"Georgia . . ."

"This was my favorite book you ever read to me, Nan. It will always remind me of you."

"Oh, sweet girl, those are some of my best memories. You in your pigtails and nightgown snuggled up with me on the sofa. I love it. I absolutely love it. Thank you."

She ran her hand over the front and the back and carefully flipped through the pages.

"So?" I asked.

"So . . . ?"

"Well, I may not have pigtails anymore, but I would still love to hear you read. It *is* Christmas night after all."

Nan's eyes were wet with tears. "I'd love nothing more."

Although I now had a new ending in my head—with Laurie and Jo married with kids—I would relish each word of the book that had won my heart so many years ago.

Nan pulled me close, and I rested my head on her shoulder.

She cleared her throat and began.

"Chapter One . . ."

ACKNOWLEDGMENTS

Thank you to my Lord and Savior Jesus Christ for your never-ending, all-consuming love that brings both purpose and passion to each manuscript I write. My life is yours.

Thank you to my husband, Tim Deese, who continues to set the example of unconditional love in our home on a daily basis. You are my heart.

Thank you to Kristin Avila, who listens and supports my ridiculously dramatic (and usually impromptu) story ideas while waiting in dark parking lots, eating in breakfast diners, and soaking our feet at our favorite nail salon. I love you oodles, friend!

Thank you to Britni Nash, who continually talks me off the ledge and leads me back to solid ground. Our Nutella Nights must never cease. I'm so grateful for friends who feel like family.

Thank you to Amy Matayo, who chats with me, laughs with me, commiserates with me, and most importantly, mentors me in this unique and crazy art of writing. You are fabulous, and I will never stop fan-girling over you. Ever. I heart you!

Thank you to Lara Brahms, who wins the award for most read-throughs of *A Cliché Christmas*. I love the way you discuss my characters like real people. Your texts and e-mails are my delight!

Thank you to my BFFs: Kacy Koffa and Kim Southwick. For being there—before, after, and during. How did I get lucky enough to have two besties? I'm still not sure, but I'd never trade either of you. You're my constants.

Thank you to my wonderful family—the Thomases and the Deeses—and to my faithful friends, who are scattered all over the world. Your encouragement, love, and support have meant so much to me this last year. Your comforting arms have been my anchor as I've grieved the loss of my baby sister, Aimee Thomas, who died on November 25, 2013, in a car accident. I love each of you deeply.

Thank you to my beta readers: Amy Matayo, Ashley Brahms, Breana Lewis, Britni Nash, Jennifer Fromke, Kacy Koffa, Kimberly Crank, Kim Southwick, Kristin Avila, Lara Brahms, Nicki Davis, Nancy Kimball, Rebekah Zollman, Renee Deese, Tammy Gray, Varina Denman. You complete me. (Insert cheesy smiley face here.)

And last, but by no means least, thank you to my readers. You inspire me to write stories from my heart by allowing me the opportunity to win yours each time you pick up one of my books. Thank you for taking a chance on me once again. I'm forever in your debt.

SPECIAL THANKS

Thank you to my editors: Georgia Varozza for an awesome first read-through edit, and Kristin Mehus-Roe at Girl Friday Productions for her expertise and time as she worked out the kinks so this final product could shine.

Thank you to Tammy Faxel and Dan Byrne at Waterfall Press for one of the best phone calls of my life. Your words of validation and enthusiasm for my future as an author are forever etched upon my heart. I'm humbled and honored to be working with such an amazing publishing house.

Thank you to my agent, Jessica Kirkland at The Blythe Daniel Literary Agency, who is one of the greatest and multifaceted blessings in my life to date. Your wisdom, your determination, your attention to detail, your faith-filled heart, and your encouraging friendship are just a few of the reasons I'm honored to be represented by you.

Bibliography

Alcott, Louisa May. *Little Women.* Boston: Roberts Brothers, 1869.

ABOUT THE AUTHOR

Nicole Deese is a lover of fiction. When she isn't writing—or daydreaming about writing—she can be found curled up and reading on a sofa. She often fantasizes about "reading escapes," which look a lot like kid-free, laundry-free, and cooking-free vacations. A girl can dream, right?

Her debut novel, an inspirational contemporary romance, *All For Anna*, has hit multiple milestones since its release in January 2013, including a 4.7 star rating on Amazon and more than 150,000 downloads on Kindle. She has since completed the Letting Go series and is elbow-deep in a new series featuring both sisterly love and swoonworthy romance.

Nicole lives in Frisco, Texas, with her hunk of a husband, Tim, and her two rowdy boys, Preston and Lincoln.